Forty South Short Story Anthology 2020

THE ELEVEN BEST ENTRIES FROM THE TASMANIAN WRITERS' PRIZE 2020

Selected by

DON DEFENDERFER CAMERON HINDRUM LIAN TANNER

40

COVER IMAGE:
Lake Dobson by Steve Barker

© 2020
Copyright remains with the individual authors.

ISBN: 978-0-6489727-3-0

All rights reserved.
No part of this book may be reproduced or transmitted
in any form or by any means, electronic or mechanical,
without the permission of the relevant author.

These are works of fiction and the characters and events
are fictitious and any resemblance to persons living or dead
is purely coincidental.

Editor: Chris Champion
Layout and design: Forty South Publishing Pty Ltd.

Publisher: Forty South Publishing Pty Ltd,
Hobart, Tasmania.
fortysouth.com.au

Printer: IngramSpark

Contents

The Tasmanian Writers' Prize

The Tasmanian Writers' Prize began in 2009 and, in order to promote and support writers, each year Forty South has published the winning story in *FortySouth* and produced an annual anthology of the best entries. Since 2014 the competition has been themed on the concept of 'island' and is open to residents of Australia and New Zealand.

WINNERS OF THE TASMANIAN WRITERS' PRIZE

2009 (2010 anthology)	John Hale (TAS)	Ferry
2010 (2011 anthology)	Leigh Swinbourne (TAS)	Away
2011 (2012 anthology)	Kate Esser (TAS)	Crossing water
2013	Debi Hamilton (VIC)	Mud flats
2014	Polly Whittington (TAS)	The chimney pot
2015	Rachel Leary (VIC)	A concrete Aborigine
2016	Craig Cormick (ACT)	No man is an island
2017	Jennifer Porter (VIC)	The Reverend
2018	Melissa Manning (VIC)	Boy
2019	Greg Burgess (TAS)	Pilgrims
2020	Andrea McMahon (TAS)	Damselfly

To order copies of the anthologies or to view other
Forty South Publishing titles visit:
fortysouth.com.au and go to our FortySouth Bookshop
Email: accounts@fortysouth.com.au
Post: PO Box 168 Lindisfarne TAS 7015

The judges

DON DEFENDERFER has been infatuated with Tasmania's natural environment since first visiting the island in 1982. He has lived in Launceston for more than 30 years. Don was State Coordinator for Landcare Tasmania for many years. This job allowed him to be inspired not only by the beauty of the Tasmanian landscape but also by the many people that are working to repair and renew it.

Don is a regular contributor to *Forty South*. He has published three volumes of poetry, co-authored a book on a wilderness area in Alaska, and has had his work published in major publications such as *The Weekend Australian* and *The New York Times*.

CAMERON HINDRUM lives in Launceston, teaches English and writes. He has produced a novel, two collections of poetry and two professionally produced plays, and this year he will complete his Doctorate in Creative Writing through the University of Wollongong. Until 2019 he was Director of the Annual Tasmanian Poetry Festival. During this period of isolation, he is offering Poems from Isolation — live poetry readings via Facebook, twice a week. Visit the Poems from Isolation Facebook page for more information.

LIAN TANNER's first picture book, *Ella and the Ocean*, illustrated by Jonathan Bentley, won the 2020 NSW Premier's Award for Children's Literature. Lian is the best-selling author of three fantasy trilogies for children, *The Keepers*, *The Hidden* and *The Rogues*, and her novels have been translated into 11 languages and won two Aurealis Awards for Best Australian Children's Fantasy. Her latest book, *A Clue for Clara* (a detective story starring a very determined chook), was published in August 2020.

Foreword

Here are some beautifully considered histories that you can hold in your hand.

The notion of what should constitute a history, especially within the parameters of the short story form, will (and perhaps should) always be hotly contested. The stories in this collection work to refract time and memory in compelling ways — and in doing so, they also serve the connecting thread of this year's competition, that of "an island or island-resonant theme". The inherent invitation to dynamic interpretation underscores these stories and there is much satisfaction found in considering the ways in which this year's anthologised writers have imbued their work with such literal or metaphorical resonances.

When 65 stories were submitted to this year's competition and judged, we had barely the beginnings of an understanding of the pandemic that has since come to define this year. It seems fitting therefore that many of these stories have innate things to say about isolation, or about resilience. It is close enough to cliché to suggest that writers require isolation in order to embrace their muse more than perhaps practitioners of any other art form — but even so, of course, there may be a sound difference between choosing it and having it mandated for the greater public good. So, again, we can be grateful for the histories inherent in this collection, for they speak to us of a time before things changed in ways that we will be a long time coming to understand.

This year's winner, "Damselfly", impressed judges with its ironic economy — in just over 1,500 words, Andrea McMahon deftly navigates and dissects a momentous decision in a focused, symbolic and honest story. Its narrative concentration exemplifies the unique nature of the short story to reach within experience and establish universal truths resulting from moments of intimate revelation. "Keaton" (highly commended) is a directly contrasting work, establishing a sweep of time and place against which human activity, even in the depths of drama and despair, seems humbled.

We were impressed as judges with some of the playful and inventive stories that are collected here, stories that work against themselves in compelling ways and serve to remind us just what an intricate edifice literature is capable of building. For all the flights of invention, of finely crafted language, of perfectly realised moments of pain and wonder and love, these stories all present truths, whether we always welcome them or not. And in that, they are indeed the most satisfying collection of histories.

I thank my fellow judges, Lian Tanner and Don Defenderfer, for their collegial wisdom, honesty and insight. I also commend Forty South Publishing for continuing to support writing within Tasmania and beyond, and for providing opportunities for success and publication that this anthology represents. Writing will always allow us to remake the world and our place in it, and opportunities to embrace this may never be more important than in the years to come.

—Cameron Hindrum

ANDREA McMAHON writes short stories for adults and children, poetry, and the occasional essay. Her short story collection, Skin Hunger, was published by Ginninderra Press in 2008 and her work has appeared in the Forty South Short Story Anthology in 2012, 2015 and 2016. McMahon lives in Hobart and works as a librarian and adult literacy coordinator with Libraries Tasmania. She has recently begun working on a novel based on the unsolved murder of her grandfather, Edgar Geer, in Hobart in 1953. More of Andrea's writing can be found at andreaswriting.wordpress.com.

Damselfly

ANDREA McMAHON

Vincent is resting on one of the many park benches dotted along the canal, his gaze tracking the brilliant blue damselflies flitting in and out of the reeds. He has taken a sip from the single bottle of beer he has pulled from the sports bag by his side. He is enjoying the warmth of a perfect summer evening, the familiar scents of his childhood.

For a week now he has been coming down to the canal each evening, not only to relax but to practice his English. From the flags fluttering on the bows of the moored barges and cruisers, it seems that today the port is full of travellers from afar, Australians and New Zealanders escaping the southern hemisphere winter. He will wander past their lovingly renovated *luxe motors* and *tjalks* when he has finished his beer. He will offer greetings in his stilted but perfectly adequate English and open himself up to learning about the many trials and tribulations of owning a canal boat.

It is the Australians whose attention he wants to attract. Once he has heard all about the leak in the bilge or the newly renovated saloon, he will direct the conversation to the wildlife: the kangaroos and koalas, the possums and platypus. Easy enough to do. Australians, he has discovered, are rather proud of their odd-looking animals. The words *marsupial* and *monotreme* are two recent additions to his English vocabulary.

For Vincent had planned to emigrate to Australia. Once he had proved himself to be of good character. This is the fantasy he had shared with his sister, Lise. She had told him about the Australian government's Family Reunion Scheme for people with no close family in their country of birth. There had been no need for him to mention the stumbling block of his criminal record. She had been visiting him in prison at the time.

They will understand, she told him, *you were young. You were protecting your brother.*

They will not understand. For he killed a man. A good man. A husband, a father. A brave man who had taken them by surprise, fighting back as two black-clad strangers in balaclavas, one wielding a hunting knife, attempted to rob a small *tabac* of the day's takings. The irony of it was that he had only gone along with his drug-fuelled brother's insane plan because he hadn't wanted anyone to get hurt. He knew how his brother could fly into a blinding rage at the slightest provocation. *He knew.*

The plan had been for Vincent to keep watch near the entrance, armed with the knife to ward off passers-by, while Antoine ransacked the till and stockpile of cigarettes. The *tabac* owner would be immobilised by fear. It would be over in a blink of the eye. They would make their get-away and he, Vincent, would forget it had ever happened because the following week he was leaving for college. He was leaving forever. Antoine was beyond help and in her ignorance and denial, so too was his mother. But his plan — hatched the moment he had seen the madness, the pure, unadulterated madness in his brother's eyes — had imploded like a house of cards when it came into contact with reality.

The *tabac* owner had not frozen at the sight of the knife. *Fight, flight, freeze, faint,* the four responses to fear that he had learned about in his psychology class. Why had it not occurred to him that they would come face to face with a fighter? That two fighters would come face to face with each other. For he was a fighter. When he had seen the baseball bat being pulled from behind the counter, when he had seen it coming down on his brother's skull he had lunged forward, uttering a primal scream, a war-cry, as the blade of his knife lodged in the *tabac* owner's neck. The same neck the man's young children had nuzzled for comfort; the same neck the man's wife had smothered with love.

He had called the emergency services, cradling his slumped brother in his arms. Wanting him to live; wanting him to die. Three weeks later Antoine was gone, having never regained consciousness. The storekeeper was pronounced dead when the paramedics arrived. Vincent, just turned eighteen, was sentenced to fifteen years in prison for manslaughter. He served six.

Vincent's reminiscing is cut short as his attention is caught by a damselfly, a glittering sapphire amongst the reeds, carefree and free. But it is no more a free spirit than I am, he thinks wistfully. We are both bound to this waterway, to this way of life. He is thinking now of the last visitor he received prior to his release. It had been his brother-in-law, Luke, a big-boned, ruddy Australian who had met his sister while studying winemaking in Burgundy. Lise had explained the situation, apologetically, shamefaced even, on a previous visit. She had used the money inherited from their mother — all of it — to purchase a vineyard in the Tamar Valley of Tasmania. To provide for the family she and Luke planned to have one day soon. Lise had explained her decision in minute detail, as if needing to expunge her sins. But he had not been bitter. He had expected nothing and anyway, his mother had left everything to Lise for her to do as she saw fit. And she had seen fit to create a fairy tale where they all lived happily ever after. *You can become a winemaker, Vincent. You can return to La Bourgogne to study like Luke. There is a shed on our property with a bathroom and kitchen. It will be perfect for you.*

It was a perfect fantasy. Luke had seen that.

You know how much she loves you, Vincent, Luke had said, his eyes lowered. He too was ashamed by what he had to say. Vincent knew how much he was loved by his big sister. What had poured out of Lise as guilt during her vacation visits to the prison had poured into him as love. Love that had shone like a comforting night light during those many dark months he had languished in a prison cell. *It is consuming her, the guilt she feels, Vincent. Every moment of every day she is thinking about you, what to do, when to do it, how to do it. My sister needs to be able to forget about this fantasy of you emigrating to Australia. Lise believes everything is possible. It is one of the things I love most about her. She believed we could own our own vineyard and now we do...It is excellent wine, by the way. Australian wine is expensive, but excellent.* Luke smiled as he said this, a small, solemn smile. Vincent had promised Luke he would write to his sister as soon as he was released.

He has been released for more than a week now. He has written the letter. A handwritten letter. The way of the prisoner. Tomorrow he will drop it into the mailbox and it will begin its long voyage to Australia. His hopes and dreams of emigrating to Australia will begin their much shorter voyage of evaporation. In the letter he explained to Lise that *La Bourgogne* is his home. He explained that he needs to make amends for what he has done, and it is not something he can do from an island at the other end of the earth.

The irony of his situation has not escaped him. He has read about the history of Tasmania, the former British penal colony of

Van Diemen's Land. Convicts transported across distant seas for far lesser crimes than killing an innocent man. Stealing a loaf of bread, a handkerchief even. There are many in this town, not so far from the village of his birth, who would be only too happy for him to be transported for his brutal crime. But he is aware of the stark reality – the only isolated island he will ever set foot on is the one he is now marooned upon.

There can be no greater isolation, he thinks, than the isolation that is imposed upon a convicted felon, a killer, from within his own community.

But he has not told Lise any of this. He has told her instead that he is continuing to work on his English – prison had been good for that – and being fit and strong – prison had been good for that also. He has picked up some labouring work at a local building site. He told her he is hopeful that when the harvest season approaches, he will be able to pick up some work at one of the local vineyards. He told her about the gentle warmth of the Burgundian summer evening on his skin. He told her about the swallows sweeping low over the canal. If he had been writing the letter today, he might have told her about a sole damselfly that has come to rest on the water's surface in front of him.

Not sinking. Not swimming. Not flying away.

He takes a final mouthful of beer, puts the empty bottle back in his bag, stands up and stretches. He spies an elderly barge owner struggling with a gas cylinder. He will approach and offer assistance in his best textbook English.

VIVIENNE AUSTEN is a Hobart-based writer and artist. Other interests include ballet, perfume, and crying at the theatre. She has a background in blogging and writing copy, but is happiest when inventing islands.

Keaton

VIVIENNE AUSTEN

I

KEATON

Keaton Island is one hundred and fifty acres, covered in pine and bramble, grasses from another land. The native flora reaches for the sun, and grasps, loosens, is smothered. A cottage sits at its centre, the eyes shuttered, the wood creaking, stubbornly set as a final violence upon the land. The shore is sand-speckled rock, hugged by mist, remembered best by sealers whose boats were dashed upon bleak, stony outcrops that rise from the ocean. Hazardous waters, evening the odds and taking their share as the fat seals subsided back into the sea, utterly indifferent to a drowning man. Keaton was never meant for habitation, or so the stories go, and go. It is nowhere, and it is special.

...

Keaton Island was abandoned to the steady creep of blackberry for well over a decade before its caretaker arrived. The wildlife learned to burrow beneath, to pluck at berries, to make do with their unnatural habitat. Birds flocked in wide sweeps, painted the small cottage (circa

1910) with their shit, which built up a spectacular thickness over time, and ate away the paint underneath. No one could remember what colour it had been, and nobody cared to. When Hendrik was chosen as the new caretaker, he chose a stormy grey and painted it at the start of his first summer there, with the help of his girlfriend Alex, his Aunty, and a few friends from the college where he taught applied art. The rest of the weatherboard cottage was painted white, and the doors were holly-berry bright red. Over the course of that first year he planted vegetables in a built up garden bed. Broccoli and potato in the spring with Alex, between sips of iced tea and trips in his dinghy, then broad beans in early winter, when she departed permanently from his life. She took with her the television, half their cd collection, and Hendrik's reason for leaving the island three nights a week. The broccoli did very well, but the broad beans never really took.

...

As sixteen years ambled past, Hendrik put his hands to more labour than they'd ever known. He cleared, pruned, planted, reaped for his island belle epoch. Storm shutters for the windows, burning snarls of blackberry as it died back each winter, the bonfire to be tended with a cider in hand, watching the flames of reclamation. A good, small life, shrinking to no more than one hundred and fifty acres. He was never truly lonely in all the years, too grateful for the gift of custody. He grew up on the mainland, watching Keaton winking in the distance, his before he knew it. Visitors came from time to time; Aunty Faye once a fortnight, old friends might stay for a week in the summer to help with weed control and drink red wine beneath the silent stars. It didn't seem to matter when the weather turned, and he'd be stuck home with no company, no news of the world. He'd read weathered paperbacks by the fire, make a stew with winter vegetables. No matter the season, there was work to be done, and with that came peace, comfort. Scents of the island brought associations. Crushed native pepperberry — a promise of sated appetite, damp soil — hard work with rich rewards. He knew the island and all it had to offer, until quite suddenly, he didn't know it at all.

II
HENDRIK

A day begins. Jam, bread, eggs and the first fire of the season. The rain is measured, the weather observed, a baby bramble torn up by gloved hand. When the wood is chopped, Hendrik takes the winding path for a brisk walk along the beach. The fresh air needles him, and the sky is limitless blue. Hendrik walks with long, swift strides as strolling is for the evenings. The surface of the water is glassy today, inviting to the senses. He responds, stops to look and sees a sleek dark something in the water. He opens his mouth as if to remark, but there is no one here to listen. Squinting does nothing to improve his vision. A seal seems most likely, but at this distance he can't make sense of its shape. He needs to blink, but knows with bone-deep certainty that the moment he closes his eyes it will be gone. His eyes begin to water; the sun is too bright. When he blinks, once, twice, a tear falls. There is nothing to see now. For a mad moment he is tempted to shed his clothes and swim out to meet it. He can't. He is not that type of person, it seems all his madness was spent in the act of moving to the island. He is mild now, he goes to bed alone at nine. He walks on.

. . .

As a child, Hendrik enjoyed art classes best of all. It was no surprise to the Aunt who raised him, when he became an art teacher. He wasn't sure whether it was luck, or a lack of talent, but he never had great success with his own paintings. A few hung in local galleries, the pride of which dulled over time as they rarely sold. A lack of ambition softened the blow. Teaching eighteen-year-olds practical techniques was a different challenge, as he wondered whether he ever saw the world with their eyes. The future spread before them, golden, and seemingly without borders. Oils were his chosen medium, and during spates of painting he would stink of methylated spirits. His fingers would be stained for weeks on end. He's stop combing his hair or shaving, become monosyllabic and impatient. He couldn't stand to be asked any questions; it was too difficult to choose tea or coffee when half of him was in the paint. It's a difficult joy for an artist. When the caretaker position was advertised, he felt it was time to do something different. On Keaton he sketches weathered trees in charcoal, the same views again and again.

. . .

He arrives back at the cottage after a half hour or so, to find an open door. As the sole occupant of the island he never bothers to lock the door, but it always careful to shut it so the wildlife don't take the opportunity to make themselves at home. In this moment he is lonely. There is no one to walk in with, and like a child he wishes he could wait for someone else to take this fear from him. The wind, he says, though the day is still. The shifting of wood, the very old door, but there is no certain answer. With no other option, he crosses the threshold. Half of his books have been pulled from the shelves, the kitchen in disarray, a jar of honey lays stickily oozing on its side. Nothing seems to be missing. In the quiet corners of his mind he imagines a line of red thread connecting the pooling of honey and the broken surface of the water. The events of the day have yet to arrange themselves into a comfortable or likely narrative for the conscious mind. He picks up his books, and cleans up in the kitchen. He eats an apple, and then he stands at the garden gate with his hands in his pockets. He looks to the plantation pine, an artificial woodland, across a small field of lavender. I will go back to the stony beach, he thinks, walking through his old footsteps, never recognising the new ones that fit so perfectly within his own.

...

Hendrik has not been sleeping well. For a week or more he has woken in the witching hours, suddenly, to nothing. Some nights the wind howls, it has become his lullaby, his home speaking words of comfort. He is deaf to the crash of possums on the roof, to the rattling of windows. What has woken him seems to come from within; by dawn it is forgotten. He remembers this now, as he picks his way through the scrub and onto the stony shore. There is a call he hasn't answered, and it drives him, stumbling blind to the water's edge. His eyes look with too much desperation, straining to see. Far beyond his sight, a tail splashes playfully, a snout breaks the surface. He feels it there, without seeing, without hearing.

...

By midday he is sitting, propped against a rock and waiting for something to happen. The sun licks him intimately, the unseasonable heat of it making his lids grow heavy. He wonders how long he can stay here — it's been two hours and his patience seems untested. When Hendrik was eight years old, his parents died in a car accident. He missed them in fits and starts, conscious of his loss at school, hiding his burden from his Aunty Faye when he moved in with her. Somewhere along the way he learned that he had in fact put mourning off indefinitely; I will cry when the time is right to do so. This too, is just beyond the horizon. He closes his eyes. He opens them.

III

HER

Her eyes are some shade of ocean, resting between blue and green, though she has never seen them for herself. Through these eyes she looks and looks, breathes and drinks and eats the scene before her. This is not a young man, and not quite an old man, which presents a question. What kind of feast is this? The old story has been reversed for her; it is she that has come upon a sleeping form, and she will be the thief. She's been inside his house with its many small items that she touched and took apart, she found nectar and drank it, and in his bed she scavenged the scent of him. Before she can nibble at his fingers, his eyes open. These too, are ocean eyes. Blue, pale, warmer waters.

. . .

I would take your hand, and you would follow me. Down, down, go deep with me and know the taste of brine and the fading light. Goodbye, the blue overhead. Ride the currents, see how sleek I shimmer, and let the salt fill you up. Do you want to know me? I fly, the currents, and out of your grasp I go. I hear the whale-song, and the song of motors, and the song of voices on the shore. When I go, I dissolve in the sea foam and have no grave. But I am watching you, from the corner of my eye as you go by. I sing you to death now, I take you to my home. I put on my coat. Faster, faster I go. Shiver and ripple, and away I go!

. . .

She isn't sure how this has happened. She had her story, and began to sing her plan to him. He didn't run because he didn't understand. He took in her nakedness and looked away, then wrapped her in his shirt and shame, and took her back to his home. She left her other self neatly folded behind some rocks where he did not think to look, but somehow he has stolen her just the same. He sits her by a warm place; she bares her belly to it, bathes. He brings her things to eat, and they are mostly strange and terrible. He asks many questions, and holds her hand. Here is book, here is painting, here is socks. She shows him: here is kiss, here is tear, here is a song to sing you to sleep. She hides her teeth- he will be just as fresh tomorrow. She thinks that he is very lonely, and she pities him.

. . .

He thinks she might be mad. He doesn't say so, but she can tell in the way he arranges her carefully and furrows his brow at her. He frets like a mother with pups, to make her safe. He also thinks she is harmless, blameless, proves it with his back to her. She'd like to sink her teeth into the tender spot at his throat, and she would save the long bones of his legs to gnaw on in lean times. There are so many lean times now. No one comes to the water's edge to take the chance, to find a sea bride, and she is mistaken for her cousins. Clap for us, catch a fish! The memory of a man's taste is threadbare when she conjures it, lost before it reaches her tongue. This one is lean, and she will fatten him up before she takes her meal.

. . .

In the cold season they learn each other's bodies through most of the daylight hours, and sleep through the long, dark nights. He likes meat, so she learns to rub it with herbs and cook the life from it. Piles of potatoes for him, slathered buttery bread. He chews with gratitude, and it's most pleasant to watch. She won't follow him to the beach in case they are seen, and he won't ask her in case she is lost where he found her. She can't make sense of all his words, but tries, and he tries too — though with less effort. As time goes on she sees that an offer made once won't be made again. He is never gone for long, and brings her fresh whole fish when he returns, live in a bucket. He leaves the room while she eats them, and she learns through his gaze that this is an ugly thing she does. He enjoys her best when she is sleepy, nuzzling, or crying softly by the window. He feeds her honey too, and combs her hair. He reads to her, the books he thinks are important. Sometimes she is listening, sometimes she is thinking of home.

. . .

Her favourite days were with her sisters, playing for hours in vast open waters. Sometimes they spoke of the changing waters, and the growing silence, though there was no need to use words. They knew each other blindly, and did not surprise each other. The coldest water was the best, the places where terrible fortune could steal any dream, where all creatures might hope to be equal. At night they lifted their faces from the water to see the stars could be very far, or very close, and they were never to know. Perhaps what separated her from the others was her desire to know, to find some safety in the answer, or learn its danger firsthand.

. . .

She does not want his Bruce Springsteen and his bad desires. She doesn't want his Paul Kelly, his Tom Waits. She communicates this to him with fierce eyes. She is thin, living off honey and red wine, and the plants he gives her make her sick. She howls when he leaves on a boat to buy supplies. Do not go where I cannot follow you. He returns with many smells, and holds her too tightly, covers her with his lack of understanding. She misses him till the moment he returns and like a child she is swamped by the confusion of a life she doesn't understand. Like his island, he tends her, but with the opposite purpose. For Keaton he plants saplings that belong, for her he has the alphabet, and pieces of lace. At night she wakes and hears her sister's calling for her; they always have been, but she'd forgotten how to listen. She remembers now, why she came ashore.

IV

ISLAND

Out where the fog kisses the water there are islets of rock, where seals warm their bellies and consider life without much judgement, save for one or two which look with interest on the rare occasion that a boat should go by. They are there for anyone who cares to look, with greed or wonder, and is known how one state bleeds into another. Past these rocks, these unfriendly islets, Keaton waits patiently for its next age to arrive. It is one hundred and fifty acres of new beginnings, to be met with fire, or silence, or love.

STUART BUSH-HARRIS teaches English and History to Grade 9 students in Launceston, where he lives with his wife and three daughters. He has had a short story published for the Tasmanian Microstories competition, which was developed for Tasmanian Living Writers' Week, and an audio recording of it was made available online. Stuart has also self-published a memoir of his gap year experiences in Egypt, "Bad Ambassadors", on Wattpad. He is currently working on a science fiction novel.

Disconnect

STUART BUSH-HARRIS

1F Y0U C4N R34D 7H15, 7H3N Y0U M4Y H4V3 0CD.

Troy can read Mandy's post perfectly well. He grits his teeth, plotting how to retaliate. Perhaps he could post a meme about negligent mothers. Far out, he thinks. It's only Day 3 of separation. Is this how it's done these days: trading barbs over social media? Troy puts his phone away for now, avoiding eye contact with the other parents as they wait to collect their little ones.

It confirms one thing for him: He's better off without her.

. . .

Isla skips ahead of Troy under the dappled light of the sycamores out of the school grounds. "Just walk, darling," he says, not wanting her to fall and graze her knees. She waits for him to catch up and then skips ahead again on the footpath that runs parallel to the road. Parked cars line both sides of it. As they approach Troy's shiny, black ute, which has never carried a power tool or a load of gravel in its life, he makes a sudden dash after Isla and seizes her by the hand, even though there's no traffic, and despite the fact that she's never yet wandered onto a road.

"You scared me!" she scolds, frowning.

"Well, you need to stay close to me near roads," he tells her. "Cars can come out of nowhere, and if one hits you, you might end up killed or in a wheelchair for the rest of your life!"

Conscious that there may be witnesses to this little melodrama, he glances casually around, preparing to go into damage control mode. Watching them from a porch rocker is the balding middle-aged man who lives alone in the house backing onto the school. Troy rolls his eyes and sighs loudly, expecting a sympathetic smile back, but the man just stares back blankly, judging him no doubt. Troy hurries Isla into the back of his dual-cab, slams the door shut and then walks around to the driver's side to let himself in.

Once they are both belted, he starts the car and pulls out onto the road. "How was your day?" he asks, and she begins to tell him, but Troy's mind has already wandered back to the balding man. He rewinds back to the previous day when the man was sweeping his porch and the day before that when he was taking out the bins. What kind of single man buys a house next to a school anyway? What if he's taken a shine to Isla? That's what paedophiles do: They date their victims from afar. Troy has watched enough docos to know. He makes the decision never to park at that end of the school again.

Isla's voice trails off. "Dad! Are you even listening?"

"Yeah, of course."

· · ·

Troy sits on the couch in the dim light, a glass of pinot beside him on the table, while Isla takes her turn to choose a music video on the TV. "Last song," he says. "It's nearly nine o'clock."

"Ohhh!" she moans.

Pop beats boom from the speakers, and a scantily clad teenager gyrates on the screen. Alarmed, Troy jumps up, snatches the remote controller off of Isla and pauses it.

"Hey!" she protests.

"I'm not sure about this one." He doesn't want her sexualised at her tender, young age.

"Mum always lets me watch it."

"Well, mum isn't here."

Isla crosses her arms theatrically.

"What about 'Here comes the Sun'?" he asks. "We both like that one."

"Fine!"

Troy finds the video for her and plays it.

He wants to relax, to be fully present in the moment, to simply enjoy the experience of listening to the song with his daughter, but the lyrics send him off on a tangent. Now, an approximation of his sun safety arguments with Mandy begins to play in his head.

It's only getting to 23 degrees and it's cloudy, she says.

It doesn't matter about degrees, he argues, it's the UV you've got to worry about, and UV still penetrates through cloud. We shouldn't be out in the sun on the beach in the middle of the day in summer. The Spanish have got it right: They have siestas. It's stupid Anglo-Saxon mentality that's got it all wrong.

Troy remembers vividly the day that Isla got burnt last Christmas. Mandy was being all blasé about it because the family were around. What's wrong with people? What is with this social phenomenon where people feel compelled to appear easy going during a crisis? Research suggests you only need to be burnt a handful of times to significantly increase the risk of developing a melanoma, and there she was laughing at people's jokes after dear Isla had lost one of her melanoma lives. Troy's response was appropriate and measured: He sat silently seething until well into the evening. That strain of easy going can go stick it where the sun don't shine, as far as he's concerned.

It's pretty much the same deal with global warming, he thinks. The scientists extrapolate the end of the world while a confederacy of dunces in governments the world over sweat instead over the economy.

The soap opera continues playing in his head. Now he's up to the scene in which Mandy walks out on him. She's brought home a baseball cap with a unicorn on it for Isla and says, Isn't it cute, Troy?

You've just signed us up to inadequate sun protection until that thing wears out, is his deadpan response.

Are you for real? she asks, her eyes tightening into a scowl.

If he had his way, he'd ban all baseball caps—and singlets for that matter! He decides, however, to keep his response factual: Caps offer no protection for ears or neck.

After a moment's hesitation, she says, You know, you take the fun out of everything.

It's an outrageous hyperbole. He can be fun.

You know what, Troy: How about I go and leave you to it for a few days? I'll stay at Mum's, and you can do everything your own pedantic, neurotic way.

Troy goes from about four to ten in less than a second. Go for good. See if I care.

The way her eyes widen and her lips fall ever so slightly apart tells him he's done it this time.

Maybe I will. She glances at the cap in her hand, says, I don't know why I bother, and then flings it at him. She brushes his shoulder as she storms out of the room.

Mandy would probably say his life was ruled by fear; he would simply call it being cautious and using common sense. Although they've only been apart for three days, he's gotten used to the idea of being a single parent, with only himself to answer to. He can censor what Isla watches. He can check the ingredients labels for nasties before buying for her. He can stand under trees as she climbs them, ready to catch her, without being called a helicopter parent.

The song has finished by now. Isla is yawning. He picks her up and carries her out to the bathroom where he brushes her teeth. Then he carries her into her bedroom. As soon as she's tucked up in bed, he gives her a big cuddle and kisses her repeatedly on the cheek. "I'm a kissing machine!"

"That's enough, Daddy."

He chuckles. "You know I love you, don't you?"

She nods, yawning again.

As Troy watches her drift off, he wonders whether a person ever really loves their spouse like their children, but he doesn't really want to go there, to linger long enough to reach a conclusion, like staring at the sun.

If he was with Mandy, he'd probably have another glass of wine right now, but drinking alone isn't quite the same, so he decides to call it a night.

. . .

Troy lies in the dark, secure in the knowledge that Isla is asleep and that he's conducted his before-bed ritual of safety checks. This involves him going from room to room methodically checking that all the appliances are turned off—the TV; the cooktop and oven; the iron, which hasn't been used for over a week; the router (who knows what that wireless radiation will do to a brain?) — and the lights and that every external door is closed and locked. His house is his fortress. This is about as safe as it gets for Troy.

On top of that, he loves the fact that he lives in a place that has few natural disasters. There are no volcanoes or fault lines in Tasmania, and tornadoes are virtually unheard of here. He deliberately bought a house on a hill so that he wouldn't be affected by flooding. The only thing to worry about here are the bushfires, but he has his survival plan all sorted. As well, he feels fortunate that Tassie's so isolated and cut off from the chaos of the world: the riots, the terrorism and the wars. No one's ever going to be in a real rush to nuke the place.

He wonders now about completely out-of-his control catastrophes, like comets hitting the earth. These thoughts actually give him some kind of perverse peace: There's no way he can prepare for that … or can he? How much would a bunker cost?

It's enough to get him out of bed and reaching for the laptop. A quick Internet search takes him to a page that reports that a basic wildfire shelter can be built for as little as $12,000. Bargain! By refining his search, however, he discovers that an actual nuclear bunker would cost $350,000. He'd never be able to afford that on one wage. Even if he and Mandy get back together, she'd never agree to one in a million years.

Troy slides back into bed and lies spread out on the diagonal, something which he'd never be able to do with Mandy beside him. No more snoring; no more sleep talking; no more having the doona ripped off of him in the night. Of course, there is one major bedtime drawback to separation, he realises …

Troy knows exactly what to do: He needs to shop for a replacement. He jumps back out of bed and flips open the laptop once again. In order to sign up for Courting.com, he has to create a profile. Troy uploads a selfie and then clicks generic descriptions that best describe him: age range — 35-45; musical tastes — rock, folk; favourite food — sushi; personality type — easy going. Troy presses *submit* and rubs his hands together as he waits for it to process.

Finally, he finds himself swiping images of single ladies in his local area … Nah, too pale … too many piercings … too much gum showing … Troy hesitates over the image of a pretty, brunette thirty-something. He clicks *Read More*.

A doctor … With their salaries combined, the bunker might not be such a pipe dream. He reads on. She has no children. Why not? Does she loathe them? Would she become an evil step mother or at best steal his affection from his daughter? She looks hot, so why isn't she taken already? There must be something wrong with her. She's probably totally airbrushed and in reality has false teeth and gets around on a mobility scooter.

Perhaps he's better off by himself after all: an island cut off from the social mainland; perhaps Ibsen's been right all this time: The strongest man in the world is he who stands most alone.

Muffled words seep through the walls, causing Troy to sit bolt upright, on high alert. He reaches for the cricket bat that he's been keeping under his bed since Mandy left him, but leaves it when he hears laughter. Troy wanders out into the corridor and then tiptoes into Isla's room, where she lies giggling in her sleep. Oh, bless. Instinctively, he turns to go and fetch Mandy to witness this spectacle of cuteness, but aborts as reality kicks in. A hitherto hidden consequence of divorce reveals itself to him, opening up a fault line fracture in his heart: Forever gone are the shared joys of your children.

All of a sudden, Troy finds he has sobered up from the drunkenness of his resentment. Now the reasons for reconnecting come flooding in: How could he better protect Isla once custody had been carved up? Could he really handle the prospect of Mandy swiping images of single men for *his* replacement? Isla having a stepfather one day? What was he thinking: that he could really do it better alone? Stubborn pride had blinded him. Could he really commit to impoverishing all of their futures over such trivialities?

How could he explain to people in all seriousness that it was the incident with the cap that did it?

Troy sees all too clearly now that marriage is just plain hard at times, but that doesn't mean just giving up on it. Isolation is not the answer; dialogue is. He knows what to do. He needs to make it right, to apologise, to negotiate — rather — to compromise. For a start, he could agree to let Isla wear the cap in winter, autumn and spring. He could probably go a step better and green light summer use of the cap in conjunction with a little sunscreen and not mention once his fears of putting chemicals on skin. Talk about team player!

The more he thinks about it, the more certain he is about his decision. Singledom would mean having to learn how to pay online bills, file a tax return and cook roast dinners, which have always been Mandy's domain. This way he can concentrate on his own domestic portfolio:

Health and Safety.

PAUL BUTTERWORTH has published eighteen non-fiction scientific papers in high-ranking medical journals (see works.bepress.com/paul_butterworth) before embarking on a creative writing journey. His first "win" was a short story called "Into the Unknown" (Queensland Writers Centre, Right Left Write, September 2019)). He came third in the CYA 2019 Everything's a Genre aspiring author category for "Retrograde Amnesia" — a 5,000-word short story. Paul has completed two Curtis Browne Creative short courses, three Faber Academy courses, and is hungry for more.

North Stradbroke Island

PAUL BUTTERWORTH

For the fifth night in a row, I could not sleep. I did not know why. There was no pharmacy on this isolated island, no sleeping pills, and no going back to the city. Why could I not sleep? Was it the music drifting from the small electric fan? As the blades spun, the warm air circulated in our small and hot caravan. I turned it off, the music disappeared, but the dead heat returned. So I turned the fan on, and the music resumed, louder and more transparent than before. Off, then on. Repeat. My wife was upset.

"What are you doing?"

"Can you hear that?"

"Hear what?"

I tried to concentrate. Was it INXS? It could have been Maroon Five. "Music, it's coming from the fan. Listen."

"What?" My wife sat, squinted her sleepy eyes. "Go to sleep, please."

There was nowhere to hide. No spare room, not in this little box. Three bunk beds where my kids slept, and one double bed for the wife and me. We were holidaying at North Stradbroke Island. A peaceful, serene sand island off the Queensland coast. Koalas, kangaroos, and glorious secluded beaches. Brisbane twinkled in the distance across Moreton Bay.

Voices outside. I peered out of the curtain. "They're coming," I said.

"What?"

I didn't bother responding. I clicked open the door, closed it carefully – I was convinced they had returned with the contract. Yes, there it was. A message written in yellow chalk on the concrete slab where our caravan sat. *Meet at the clothesline.* A strange place to meet the CEO of Netflix, but it wasn't as if there was a conference room at the caravan park.

We sat opposite each other. He was like a ghost – I knew he was here, but I couldn't see him. A conduit between myself and the viewing public – those who would watch and hear my story. A story of loss and confusion. A tale of one man's inability to live in reality. I was under his spell as I digitally signed the contract. It was done in a virtual reality setting – behind glasses or goggles, or a combination of both. I couldn't tell. People were watching. But they weren't really people – fairies, they were – dressed in strange little outfits, sitting in trees, watching and smiling. Some were sitting on the clothesline. Others on my shoulder, whispering weird things in my ear in a language I could not understand. It was all happening so fast, and without any input from me. I was going along with the ride and had no control over the brakes. Wait, I should have a lawyer review this! Who cares? Soon enough, the entire world would know me and my story.

I managed to open the trunk and slide into the car. I would try to sleep here until the police arrived – and they would arrive. I would be handcuffed and taken away from my family. And so I should be. I did not belong here, mingling with the normal people. I had done something wrong, but I knew not what it was. I could not go back into the caravan — it was not fair on my wife. She was trying to sleep. She was a regular person. A woman who enjoyed the outdoors and sharing it with her family. She had told me not to come.

"It might be better if you stay at home."

"No," I had said. "I will be fine. I will sleep like a baby tonight."

"You haven't slept in four days. You need to go to the doctor."

I did not like doctors. They understood nothing. Oh, you have an anxiety disorder, one had said. Another: No, no, no — it is depression. Bipolar, another had said. I tossed and turned in the back of the car. The sun began to rise. How would the police make it onto this island? Would they take the ferry from the mainland like everyone else? Did they have their own special police boat? And how the hell did Netflix get here? I knew they had recorded the meeting. It felt like an interview, but I can't remember speaking. There was a tap on the window. The kids were looking at me funny — *who is this strange man?*

My wife, she'd had enough. She opened the trunk door. "You need to go to hospital."

"What? Why?"

"You know what you have been doing all night?"

"I'll be okay."

"No, you won't. Besides, I don't want you here. You woke up the entire caravan park last night. Do you remember what you were saying?"

"Kind of."

"You think Netflix is making a documentary about you."

That sounded crazy. "Okay. You're right. I'll go."

My wife drove me to the ferry terminal. She hugged me. "Go straight to your GP. I will be calling her to make sure you arrived. Okay?"

I nodded. "I'm sorry. I don't know what is going on."

The kids waved goodbye as their mother drove them back to the campsite. Back to safety, away from their psychotic father. I walked on board. A decayed old ferry — blue interior and white exterior. The passengers spoke of a man. An unknown man. He had infiltrated the internet and crashed the system. They were all talking about him. Me. The women to my left, the teenagers to my right. They agreed — he would be caught. He had not covered his trail. He had sent an email with his name attached to it. What an idiot! He had sworn and cursed at everyone and anyone. He would be brought to justice. The people were owed justice.

The five-minute ride across the water felt like five hours. A bus took me to Cleveland train station, but where was I going? People were talking about me. The announcements over the PA system. What were they saying? Commuters eyed me with suspicion as I boarded the first train. It was going the wrong way! I got off, boarded another and headed in the opposite direction. On then off. Repeat. One hour later, I finally caught the correct train and alighted from Robina station.

I called my supervisor. "Jacqui. Something is wrong!"

I called a few others. Get to the doctor was the overwhelming advice. I did so. My GP referred me to the hospital, but all I wanted was Valium. I should not have stopped taking it in the first place. That was what I needed — Valium and sleep! I went home and spoke with my neighbour — asked him how long he had been spying on me. Why had he been dishonest? How long had he been working for Netflix? He wasn't sure.

I rode my bike in the heat. My legs were numb. So were my hands. I couldn't feel my feet. I didn't know it then — but my body had redirected all blood flow to my vital organs. I was as close to having a heart attack as a 41-year-old could get. I made it to the hospital — its size and strength frightened me. I scurried inside to escape the terror and was admitted quickly.

I got my Valium. I got my sleep — I did not return to North Stradbroke Island.

SUSAN CAMBRIDGE researches, writes and publishes historical fiction, non-fiction and short stories. Her novel Bound by Sea *relates the story of her convict and merchant ancestors in Australia. She lives in Christchurch, New Zealand, and is currently working on a collection of short stories about the strong women in her ancestry, many of whom contributed to the development of Australia or New Zealand. She is on the committee of Canterbury NZSA and studies yoga, mindfulness and dreaming.*

The voyage

SUSAN CAMBRIDGE

Elisabeth peers through swirling white. Flour dusts arms, face, neck. She brushes it off before it cakes to prickling paste, mixed with her sweat, heat rising from the ovens. As she runs to the front of the bakery, swirling skirt catches a bench, hip bumps. She rubs, imagines the bruise staining white skin, spreading like cherry juice around the bone.

Fifty years old, broad shoulders, strong arms from working a Scottish farm, she steps to the doorway of the bakery shop. Eyes, blue grey as a cloudy sea, watch morning sun tint the mountain-top above the town of Hobart. Light stains water, dances on masts of waiting ships. Smell of the sea, rope, horses, fish, rise from the town cradled by the River Derwent. She feels new-born. Freed from old constraints, she manages her own business, supports her family, caught in the weave of this growing town.

Along the street the Black Swan Hotel disgorges staggering men, eyes red with drink and lack of sleep. Kemp's store on the waterfront sells liquor imported on trading ships. Her bread soaks some of the liquor consumed by patrons.

"A quartern loaf this morning?"

"Warm bread for your breakfast?"

"We'll have hot pies tonight."

She smiles, presses loaves into waiting hands. Her daughters bustle and chat. The baker slaps bread on benches, shakes the counter with his hammering. The sound is a bell calling passers-by to action. Ovens sweat heat. Sweet smell of yeast bubbling with sugar heralds brown crusts, soft melting dough inside. Best flour, Elisabeth sees to that, long experience of grains. Millers beware, she'll notice any added corn or husks.

Van Diemen's Land society in 1824 has layers like the tilled soil at home in Ayrshire. Elisabeth picks through it like a red billed gull finding levels of sustenance. Convicts, ex-convicts, children of convicts, colonial settlers who think themselves "quality", and soldiers: officers and men. There are visitors too: sealers and whalers, traders, explorers, adventurers. Elisabeth's bakery serves loaves to anyone who enters, money in hand.

Two months since she arrived. The first weeks in the settlement she sought information on where there was a need, a gap to fill. She's used to practical solutions, mender of fences, patcher-up of holes.

...

"Opportunities," Robert says as he shows her leaflets, posters. "Opportunities, adventure, a new beginning. Can't pass that up."

Robert of the Aird they call him for the place of their land in Ayrshire. Blue eyes sparkle above his beard. She finds herself caught in the web of his charm, enthusiasm. Together for 27 years, she's borne him nine children. His 17 years' seniority, 67 to her 50, makes no odds, nor that he had a wife before, another family.

The papers he brings flash gleeful hyperbole until her head aches: "Opportunities." "Climate equal of any in the world." Visions of land lying uninhabited, there for the taking. But in quieter moments alone in her kitchen she sees an abyss dark and rocky open before her. All the detail of the venture will rest with her. Wide ideas for Robert, practicalities for her. Always been that way.

He gathered her in all those years ago, straight, tall, strong, with land, a farm breeding cattle, growing crops. They worked and loved and raised their children. This is a time when many would feel deserving of a rest. Sons to take on the farm, grand ideas put to bed.

He needs a challenge, proof he's still a man of action. Who is she to deny him that? Truth be told one part of her quivers with excitement: new interests, challenges, a chance to prove herself. The gentle rolling hills of Ayrshire are printed in her bones, but even she can see in the 1820s that opportunity declines. Where will they find farms for sons, men with assets for their daughters? Land, she knows is all.

Robert and his sons unite over this adventure, oppose her tentative objections. Robert corals them in his paddock. She faces them like one of their docile cows yapped at by the dogs. Van Diemen's Land, a foreign-sounding name, exotic. Might be an island fantasy invented by desperate convicts, wanderers, explorers.

Elisabeth wants solid facts. "How would we get there?" "How do we get grants of land when we arrive?" "What should we take?" Robert has answers, talks cousins, nephews, into taking part, uses charm, persuasion. She's not immune either, even after all these years.

Then he unleashes his latest idea: purchase a ship to carry family and stock, sail it to the island across the world. Words bat about her head, trapped gulls, beaks open for pecking or breathless wonder. She stands silent, shaking.

...

"She's a fine brig." *Amity* floats, dwarfed by the hills, on the water of Stranraer Harbour. Robert puffs out his chest, proud as one of her hens, an egg just laid, or maybe the rooster crowing to bring his flock to heel. "Only seven years old. Built in New Brunswick."

Elisabeth looks at the little ship, two masts, long bow-sprit, round and sturdy, decks shrunk by distance to the size of the family dinner table. She'd thought of a ship wide as a farmyard. This *Amity* is tiny. How will it hold children, animals, farming machines?

"She's big enough, 148 tons. Built to withstand winter storms in the North Sea, should cope with the seas in the south." Elisabeth puts her hand to her stomach. She's heard of giant blue rollers driving through oceans filled with ice.

The letter arrives from the office of the Secretary of State for Colonies, Downing Street in London. Parchment crackles in her hand, gives off a smell of ink, officials in musty suits, dusty offices. She takes a breath, drops it to the table as if it burns her hand. This makes it real. Permission is given, as requested, for Robert Ralston to proceed to Van Diemen's Land with his wife, two sons, six daughters. The letter asks the lieutenant-governor, Colonel Sorell, to grant Robert and his sons land in proportion to the means he may have of bringing it into cultivation.

"I must show I have capital: five hundred pounds I believe, and the same for each of the sons who get land."

Elisabeth feels a jolt like lightning to her skull. It's really going to happen. "Lot of money."

"We can find it."

Robert persuades a partner, Mr Greig, to help fund the cattle he'll take, works on cousins to join the ship as passengers, Elisabeth hears his enthusiasm igniting sparks. Their sons are alight with excitement, changing minds about who will come, who stay to finish schooling.

She sighs as a dog barks, cows moan in the night, dreams of lists: food for the voyage, clothes. Who knows what they might need? Her daughters help, capable young women. She cannot think beyond readying the ship, cannot encompass thoughts of what it will mean to leave or what awaits when they arrive.

Shimmering mist cloaks the harbour in silver and gold. She watches the animals gather: four cows and two bulls, more cattle, horses, sheep, two pair of fox hounds. "Good hunting they say, catch your own food, those kangaroos." She imagines them hopping, great tails, dogs snapping, teeth on skin. "Rather eat bread. Take machinery Robert for harvesting crops."

The threshing machine is a tangle of metal and wood, a monster of modern technology. She helps Robert find a captain for the ship, two officers, merchant navy, eager for adventure, opportunities.

The cabins are small. A chest of drawers, a table, cots built into walls. The animals get the best of the space. "Good breeding stock, make our living." The four dogs have the run of the ship.

She packs oats into barrels, salt meat, malt and soup for prevention of scurvy. Butter, potatoes, onions go on top to use at the start. "We can buy fresh food in Dublin, at Rio, at the Cape." A cow will give milk to moisten porridge. The older daughters find fabrics, scissors, thread. Elisabeth packs recipes for bread.

A maid, a cook, a herdsman to care for the cattle, agree to seek adventure. Sons Matthew and John, will travel, Gavin and William stay behind, possibly follow later.

Cattle hoisted aboard, food stored, hay for the animals, she checks the lists. Captain William McMeckan paces the deck, supervises loading. She sees his fingers grip the ropes, the rail. At sea only his skill with frail timber, canvas sails, hand of God, will keep them safe.

November 1823, a cold wind ripples Loch Ryan. Elizabeth thinks of the wild Irish Sea, rain hissing on white spray beyond the sheltering arms of the loch. "Is it wise to leave in winter?"

Robert strokes his beard. "Reach the south in the summer. Stop in Rio, round the Cape of Good Hope in February or March. Winds are best then; summer down there."

On the day of departure Elisabeth stands on the deck, feels her life unmoored. Those brown-green hills were part of her soul. Now she's cut free, anchor pulled up, few possessions, only her family. Freedom is a sword with double edges: loss as well as gain. Her mind is empty, numb. A daughter beside her takes a breath, lets out a sob. Wind brushes tears on her cheek, flings them to mingle with salt spray.

Later she feels the bow rise to the first of the swell. The animals moan, timbers creak. She lifts her arms to the wind, feels she could fly, a weight gone from her shoulders. She belongs to no country, floats at the mercy of God, wind and tide, all of this tiny world within her reach, decisions constrained for the moment to the ship and people on her decks.

. . .

Hobart, March 1824: she stands at the rail, looks on cottages blowsy with autumn flowers, a town at the foot of a mountain, held in the arms of calm waters of the River Derwent. Peace strokes her soul after storms in the Southern Ocean. She felt little *Amity* tested to the end of her strength, more than once wondered if the breath of salt and icy water might be her last. Little time to worry, she had to comfort children, look to the welfare of the animals, make sure humans and stock were fed and watered, even as fear froze her to the bones.

The town looks temporary: timber dwellings, one or two stone buildings by the port, homes for beings from another planet, shelter for a week, a night. She thinks of the square stone tower of the Castle of St John dominating Stranraer as she departed, settled in the landscape for three centuries. Her own stone farm house was home to generations. For a moment the stone in her belly threatens to drag her into despair.

Curiosity rouses her to action. She sees the colours, near hills green, those further off blurred in an overlapping haze of blue. The country feels melancholic, wrapped in danger, alien to one used to warm brown Scottish hills. Light is bright, makes her eyes ache, birds call, harsh sounds rebounding from the mountain into distant shuddering wilderness where who knows what beasts walk.

She finds they're expected, destination reported by a ship captain met at the Cape. In the wide streets, people stop to chat, eager to greet a newcomer. She watches, listens, keen to find out what they lack that she and her family might provide. Talk is of the hanging. One of five convicts escaped two years before from the island prison in the west will meet his end. "Ate his companions, lost in the forest, no food. Ate one another. He was the last alive."

Her stomach clenches. What men, what evils lie in that blue yonder? Has God deserted this island? Is she no longer in his care, having left her own land, a wanderer like Moses in the desert?

Bustle of ships, sealers, whalers and traders, carts from the up-river settlements, leaves her giddy, bemused. They pen the animals ashore to await allotted land.

"Governor Sorell's leaving." Robert's shoulders slump. "Recalled. The lady he lives with is not his wife, has a husband back in Britain. Someone complained. Colonial Office had to act. Bad example."

"Your letter's no use then?" Elisabeth curbs her anger, clenches a fist. One of her careful details gone astray.

Robert has the grace to look ashamed. "Have to go to Sydney, ask Governor Brisbane there to confirm the land grants. He's in charge overall. Better chance of selling *Amity* in New South Wales." Elisabeth nods, lets her hand unclench. Make the best of it.

Furled sails, masts forlorn, *Amity* has been her home, her place of safety for five months. She feels as she might farewelling a family member or a home loved and cherished. "Can't keep her, too much capital. Need it for our land. I'll make this voyage with her, take Matthew."

Her careful questions on arrival now bear fruit. Family survival over these first months will depend on her. Bread, she has found is lacking. No one bakes good bread. There's plenty of liquor, sugar from Mauritius, wheat grown on inland farms, a mill on the hill, but women or their servants spend hours mixing, kneading, baking. Most have coins to buy a loaf if any were for sale.

She walks up the hill, out of breath after the months on board ship. Enters the flour mill, mad giant, waving its arms in defiance of westerly winds. Inside great stones grind and rumble, wheat grains between their teeth. Elisabeth trickles silky grains into her palms, rubs them, puts a dab on her tongue. She knows flour, years of growing, milling, baking. "You can grind it finer? No corn added for padding. I'll pay for best quality."

Robert leaves her half their capital for ovens, bowls, benches. She finds a man who calls himself a baker, tests his loaves. Within a month of arrival she advertises in the *Hobart Town Gazette:* biscuit, bread, quartern loaves, warm breakfast bread. She'll have pies hot from the oven in the evenings, all made from very best flour.

Reading the advertisement she finds herself salivating, feels flaky pastry on her lips, gravy, tasty as a simmered soup, warm in her mouth. The bakery will provide a shop. They brought surplus stock from Scotland: shirts, leather saddlery, hardware.

Captain McMeckan's hand is firm in hers, his two officers steadfast as trees, used their skill to guide the ship over oceans. She pats Robert's pocket, crisp with the letter she helped compose for Governor Brisbane.

Her daughters advertise their skill in dress-making, use the patterns, fabrics, cottons they stored aboard the ship. Muslin, bombazine, silk: red, green, gold, brown and useful black. Elisabeth feels herself above desire for baubles, too old for peacock colours, but she revels in this profusion scattering the rooms above her shop. Like a speckled hen in her Scottish farmyard she longs to drape herself and strut.

Women buying bread grasp at fabrics, those who come for fittings leave with loaves. And gossip. When Robert returns with *Amity* sold to the government, letters confirming land grants, a load of oranges, balls of northern sun to light the corner of the shop, she knows where the best land lies and how to farm it, keep it safe.

Land close to Hobart is long since taken. Land around the town rising in the north on the Dalrymple River has little forest, needs no clearing. Squatters already graze the plains there, water in plenty. While Robert with Matthew and John take possession of their grants, drive animals overland, she continues to support them from the bakery.

Fences, crops, a harvest, stables for the horses, finally a house. Land gives according to the labour invested in the soil. When the house is built, she joins the men at the farm they name Logan Falls not far from Launceston. Several daughters have found husbands, women on the island in short supply.

The early years are testing. Stray cattle wander, stock disappears. Shots in the night lead to bodies or wounded men: bush rangers attacking those who try for justice. Elisabeth is too concerned with farming, survival, to worry overmuch about the war between settlers, police, native inhabitants of the land. Development is all. And if she sheds a tear at the betrayal, exile of those dispossessed, women and children who in the early days received bread at her hands, it's soon lost in the care of whether the wheat has rust, or a horse is lame.

She's safe within the walls of a substantial house, respected leader of her family. Sons farm on either side, part of the local gentry, bakery forgotten. She buries Robert when he finally succumbs to death, beside the nearby church. Son John takes on the farm.

For her this was indeed an island of opportunity, a place where she came into her own, renewed her life, found a resilience she might never have discovered.

DM CAMERON is an AWGIE nominated radio dramatist, award-winning playwright and celebrated short film writer. Her debut novel, Beneath the Mother Tree *was listed as a top Australian fiction read for 2018 and long listed for the Davitt Awards. She is the author of several stage plays, including her critically acclaimed solo work,* The Flowering. *She has had four plays produced by ABC Radio National —* Water Tight, The Salt Maiden, Bringing Down the Moon *and* Shopping for Lifeforms. *Her film script of* The Salt Maiden *premiered at the 2014 Cannes Film Festival, won best screenplay and short film at the Port Stephens Film Festival, and was overall winner of the Coasties Film Festival 2015. She is a recipient of the Australian Writers Guild/Queensland Theatre Company Mentorship Scheme, a Varuna Litlink Residency and twice recipient of the Fresh Ground Scheme at the Judith Wright Centre. Find out more at dmcameron.com*

Swimming towards the sun

DM CAMERON

Elaine is tired from being woken by that strange wailing — the Muslims calling to their God or whatever. And the heat. All day the heat has been unbearable, sticking to her like a wet plastic bag clinging to her thigh, which is what happened this morning when they were snorkelling. Disgusting. The memory of it still turns her stomach. Sweat trickles, dampening her new dress. Everything is hot — even the fresh lychees she is sucking on, the juice dribbling down her wrist adding to the horror of stickiness.

Poor Robert looks hot and bothered too.

The twins have the right idea, splashing each other in the water so clear you can see where the sandy bottom ends and the reef begins.

Their strong teenage bodies broadening now at the shoulders. Her baby men. All this sun and sea will be good for their acne.

She pulls a Wet One from her handbag and wipes her wrist.

Robert hasn't touched his Gado. Flies are starting to crawl over it. She stops herself from saying something. He has been so snappy lately, she doesn't dare. Is it because of the sex thing? With all these damn hot flushes she can't be bothered anymore. He doesn't seem to mind. He never initiates anything. Thank God.

Maybe he does mind? He never says so — then he wouldn't, would he? He's beginning to go grey around the temples, poor thing. Still handsome though. She has a flash of him as a new father, one son in each arm, looking up at her, beaming that heart-expanding smile of his. She misses his smile, misses the way he once held her in the quiet hours of night when thoughts of death would creep up on her. She had always envied his ease with the great unfathomable.

He finishes his beer and signals to the waiter for another. Definitely in holiday mode. Robert always stops at one. She hopes it will lighten his mood. There he goes again with that new gesture of his — pressing his fingers against his eyes — trying to shut out the world. She swallows, remembering how she had woken with such a strange sense of foreboding. But that foreign godawful wailing would do that to anyone, wouldn't it?

The Wet One in her hand is brown and grubby now. What to do with it? There are never any bins. She tucks it under the fork at the side of her plate. The waiter can deal with it. Here he comes now with Robert's beer. Such beautiful looking people with their olive skin, and so lithe. She wonders what they're called — Lombokians? Robert would know, but she doesn't ask. There was a time when he found her ignorance funny. "You're so cute," he would say and reward her with that smile.

The sunset is really beginning to do things now. She rummages in her handbag for her phone to take a photo, then gives up. It's all too hot. Just one more breathtaking sunset, that's all. There'll be another tomorrow, and the next day no doubt. This holiday seems to be going on forever.

She glances again, in turn, at each of the volcanoes. The gigantic one in Bali and the much closer one on Lombok. Robert knows their names. She's hopeless at holding all those silly facts in her head. She remembers the term "ring of fire" though and doesn't like that fact one bit. Here they are right in the centre of it. No wonder it's so bloody hot. With climate change and all that palaver, either volcano could erupt at any minute. She prefers this side of the island, because this is the only beach from which you can see both volcanoes at the same time. She has taken to the habit of checking them on a regular basis for any sign of life. Is that smoke or mist on Lombok? Just mist. If she dwells on the knowledge that both volcanoes are active, bubbling away inside, she finds the need to return to her air-conditioned room at the hotel to be surrounded by all her familiar things and pretend she isn't here on this funny little island full of stubby tailed cats and horses pulling carts.

Robert is transfixed by the colours bleeding into the sky. "I want to separate," he says.

"Separate what?"

"Us." He looks at her then.

He is weeping.

No. Not here. Not now. With the twins. In public. "Why?" It comes out much louder than she wants as she flicks her eyes around the other tables to check if anyone is listening.

"I think it's run its course."

Its? He's referring to them as its.

The heat is stifling.

She can't breathe.

She stands.

He looks worried now. "Elaine?"

She walks forward into the tepid water toward the twins.

They stop splashing each other and stare.

"Mum?"

"What are you doing?"

"I'm too hot."

"Elaine. You're getting your new dress wet."

But the water feels so nice as she swims towards the sun — something to push against, something to hold her up. She dives under and twenty-five years of love explodes in her heart.

STEPHANIE DAVIES was born in Hobart, and splits her time between Melbourne and Tasmania. Her writing has been published by Overland, PEN Quarterly, *and* The Music. *She is a graduate of* RMIT *University.*

In the rose garden

STEPHANIE DAVIES

I peel the petals back on the Grandiflora, revealing the tightly wound bud, potpourri unspooling at my feet. The roses aren't *papier maché*. After the rain, they will rot. The windowpane is made of sand, fused into glass; anything can crack under pressure, fissures spreading.

Raindrops slash the glass, unable to penetrate. My reflection is muted, as if another face. Outside, it's just another whitewashed building. Inside there are bars, secret barricades.

A sturdy woman in a pressed uniform charges at me, her cheeks a collage of broken capillaries.

"What are you doing?" she asks crisply.

She will plough me down.

"I'm visiting Sally," I whisper.

"Have you signed the book?"

"No. I couldn't find any staff."

"Who do you think you are?"

The woman marches me down the hallway, heels clicking with military precision. The Matron badge is pinned squarely to her chest. We retrace my steps until we reach the guestbook. I skim the book to a blank page.

I write my name in the first line, linking the letters. I tease my scarf with my fingers — it's a motif of thorns like teeth.

Prisons aren't always rimmed by barbs. Not everyone locked up is lawless. But they all dream of breaking free. People forget the world outside, forget what living is: the taste of rain on a tongue, dancing in the dark without an audience.

Sally writes letters from the inside; letters to herself. She's on Facebook, but she isn't connected. We had a brief but intense friendship as children. I wanted to be like her, wilful and wild, Robin to her Batman. Sally wasn't of this world. She still talks about leaving, as if death is a vacation she can return from. I keep thinking it will happen, but she presses play again.

The sharp lines of the clinical setting don't suit her. The scatter cushions are comic in their duplicity. The room makes her harder, like she forgot how to be soft, the importance of vulnerability — of letting her guard down.

We talk in dribs and drabs.

"It's pretty here. You can see the snow on the mountain," I say. "The sun rising over the city."

She stares off into the middle distance, her hair a golden crown, her clothes shapeless velour.

I try to fill the room with words. It's hard — few topics are safe, landmines on the periphery. Work talk reminds Sally she's unfit for it. Relationships — of her desire to have one — the instinctual need to be touched, of primal things.

Sometimes Sally gets taken advantage of by men. We don't talk about that. Her family is gone. I do not speak of mine: dysfunctional but alive, flawed but loving. I point to the crab-apple tree, naked without leaves. "Do you like the rain, Sally? It's pretty in the garden."

In the past, Sally holds her hand out to me. She pulls me out of the gravel, brushing the grit from my knees. "You're all good now."

Once, we soared down Wellesley Street with glee — hearts filled with sun, rain, and sometimes the mist which drifted off the mountain. I could never keep up with her blonde pigtails flapping in the wind, her nine-year-old self perky and perfect. She was gifted, playing the violin like a pro in the youth orchestra.

Does she remember my name?

I begin again. "Do you still ride your bike up the mountain?"

Sally looks down at her hands clasped in her lap. She can't go back to who she was, she told me once in a lucid moment. It's as if she's been sentenced to a kind of death, but she's still in there. I try to be present for Sally, to see her. I'm here because I'm certain that we're all broken in our own ways, but only some of us are locked away.

After some time, Sally whispers, "Sorry my brain is fuzzy. They've put me on experimental drugs. No one has taken as many as me. I should be dead."

She stresses the wrong parts of her words. Her phonics a tell, a hint something is off.

We used to play show and tell on the Island, in our primary school classroom. Sally always had something wonderfully subversive to share, like she was laughing at the world, the classroom her stage.

"I brought you a present." The package is crumpled and sweaty in my hands. I fling it at her.

"Ta," she smiles, her eyes warm. "Do you mind if I save it till tomorrow? Nobody comes on Wednesdays. It's hump day."

I beam at her, my smile fluorescent, maybe real. "Of course. Can I get you anything else?"

"If we're good, the Matron will make us a cup of tea. I miss tea."

"Aren't you good, Sally?" I tease.

"Not always. They say I'm a problem child. They'll send me away."

"I'm sure they won't." I'm not, but it seems a folly to make promises to someone who expects them to be unkept. Someone who is broken down grains of a former self. There's a picture on the wall of Sally with a muscular brown dog with floppy ears.

"How's Jasper?" My tone is overly cheerful.

"They won't let me see him. I need good behaviour for that." Sally's eyes glaze over. She won't meet mine.

She is still beautiful, but there is something lumpy about her, like she's forgotten how to use her body, like she's decaying.

"I'm sorry, Sally. Would you like me to visit him?"

"Yeah, that would be good. I'll give you his favourite toy." She points to a ragged-looking toy on the floor.

We drink our Lipton Tea black. I envy Sally's lack of responsibility, void of milk or sugar like our tea. I peer through the bay window, through roses wilting under the weight of sleet. There are no bars on the common room, but no privacy either. Cold eyes watch us, stilting the rhythm of our chat. Personal space is a luxury Sally hasn't earned.

I leave raw, my emotions simmering beneath the surface. I need to escape the chemical smells, the damp oppressiveness and faux homeliness of this place. Out front there's a retro bicycle resting on the picket fence, one of those green enamel ones with a brown basket.

I wish Sally could see it, feel the sun on her face. I'm not sure what the rules are. Does she have basic rights? She's committed no crime — that I know of — except not playing by the rules.

That night, the violin leans against the white-metal-bedframe in my room. I don't remember how it got there. The hinges on the case are rusted, its face powdered with dust. I didn't ask Sally about it, not wanting to cause her pain.

Black roses mould outside where yesterday they were deep pink blooms. I pop the window — the ocean breeze will flush the dust out.

It's stuck.

It reeks of something rotting. Like I forgot to take the trash out. Like I'm disintegrating.

A perky woman dressed in a white uniform enters. "Would you like some tea?"

"Who are you? Are you mum's friend?"

"Yes honey. I'm taking care of you while she's gone."

I drop something on the floor. It is a scarf covered in thorns. I look at the ground. It is marble, maybe concrete; carpet receding. Out the window the mountain is black and grim, with no snow to soften its edges.

Someone else enters the room, filling the silence.

"Hello, Matron. Is my friend coming today?"

"She just left, Sally."

DÉSIRÉE FITZGIBBON is an artist, curator and teacher who lives and works at Okines Beach, Dodges Ferry. Her work as a painter, performance and textile artist is inspired and informed by place; by the rhythms and patterns inherent in the natural world. She considers her role as an eco-artist carries with it a responsibility to raise awareness of issues relating to loss of species and habitat, and her focus currently is to build community through engagement with the arts, rituals, celebrations and daily conversations. Writing is an integral part of her practice; daily journals record observations of the natural world, her pilgrimages to remote places and life on the islands of Tasmania. Writing is the tool for her deep search for meaning.

My grandmother's embroidered pocket

DÉSIRÉE FITZGIBBON

Adrift in a sea of faces, some appearing from past encounters, I cast a net, searching a word, a clever idea, a sentence strung like pearls of insight to cast at the feet of poets. The heads of writerly thinkers hold words like sand, millions of pinpoints of light massing together, forming shapes, amorphous longings, laments, joyful whoops, utterances, mumbles and echoes.

Words like sand. Sandy shorelines limned with light, rivers awash with stones, oceans deep and treacherous, words scattering now like debris to be collected by timeworn searchers of wordy woes. Woes? Jewels I say, tattered fragments of ropes, bottles washed smooth, glass and clay, fibre and remnant memories from my grandmother's pockets.

Words like oily smudges on her apron, echoing scents and tastes, teasing, titillating, tempting.

Words like pears on a late summer's day, juicy warm and sweet, clothes flapping from wooden pegs, cavorting in the salty wind from the straits, jars filled with butterscotch, jars filled with feathers and bones.

Words like keys, piano keys yellowing like the teeth in my grandmother's smile, gaps like cadences in a Bach fugue.

Words like gaps.

There's a word fitting this memory moment, words hugging her body like a worn and comfortable flowery frock, yet so many gaps, markers around the gaps pointing to absence.

Catching words in nets. Stitching nets over holes, embroidering my grandmother's apron pocket to better hold the stories firm and fast.

Doris lived alone on a small island in the Strait, the Island of the Moonbird some call it. Every year she watched the exhausted birds return from the north, flying thousands of kilometres to their nests on the shores of the islands, heralding the time to plant summer crops and every year she awaited the shearwaters' departure for the northern summer, marking time on her map of seasons.

She lived a simple life, moving between two huts, spending her dreaming nights in a tiny wooden hut at the end of the snaking pathway in her seven acre garden. Her light came from a kerosene lamp, a light to read by, kept company by moths and nocturnal critters who gazed with day blind eyes at her straight backed form; beside her a gnarled stick rested on a pillow, the radio tuned to ABC World News. Her heat in winter thrummed from the wood burning stove from which emerged fragrant rustic loaves of bread, puddings and pies, long simmered legs of mutton.

Her garden was alive with drought resistant flowers, bees, skinks, possums and wallabies. Cape Barren geese flocked overhead, honking and heralding another seasonal shift. Magpies carolled early morning, time to get up time to get up.

Her life unravelled from the basket of floral garments and knitted cardigans she kept in a corner of her night time hut. "Tell me about this one," I begged as I drew the '50s frock from beneath her favourites. They were timeworn, darned with coloured threads, mended and nurtured like the stories we shared, mended through the needle of care and the weaving of nets.

Words like nets. She netted me with her stories; held me captive. The frock was bought in a thrift shop near her back packer accommodation in Nelson, New Zealand. "I remember that one," she twittered, perched that day on her bed near the open window. The story meandered along hemlines of willow-lined lanes and floated on clear glistening streams, bubbled up from river rocks, tripped over faded memory tracks as she recalled the day she bought it, the exact date, close to her birthday, how thrilled she was to have a new frock to wear!

She rolled along all her youthful days in the town where she lived before the winds of the fates carried her to the island. Stories of lost loves and found, of harsh windswept shores where she collected driftwood for her stove, stories to make an 85-year long life as layered and intricate as an archaeological dig. I came with my spade and torch, we entered the caves together, journeying into the deep past.

Suddenly, one afternoon as I drifted along, in the midst of her opus, my eyes alighted on a tiny white nest on the window sill. A friend had brought the nest in, having discovered it on the dirt track. I was amazed at the fragility and whiteness of it. The nest had been woven meticulously from the hair she pulled from her brush — she cleaned it daily, leaving sparse mounds of fibrils on the sill from where her wee feathered visitor collected them and set about making a hollow home to hold smooth, pregnant eggs.

Doris excavated her next glimmer of golden thread as the wrens in the garden darted between stick-like branches of the shrubby undergrowth. One perched on the edge of a nest, a cup hanging precariously, encased in cobwebs. An ancient tree sent roots out from a sturdy trunk, rusting buckets nearby were set firm to catch drips of rainwater weeping from fretting pipes hanging mid-air from the roof of the hut. An hour passed like light through a lens, bleaching the blanket of her dreams.

The leaves are falling, the music of the wind entangles with the raucous metallic shriek of the cockatoos as they flit through the garden, interrupting the space. The wrens move off with quick darting gestures, startled and wary, then return. The moment of reverie is lost now, another frock, another story to retrieve from the basket on another day.

I stealthily tucked the stories into the pocket of my grandmother's apron, collected them like precious, rare shells. They nestled there and sat comfortably alongside the stories of the animals we encountered on our holidays on that Bass Strait island. We fondled and examined them over and over as we sat under the stars or by the hearth, yarns of wombats, pigmy possums, echidnas and rare albinos we considered gifted or special. We laughed anew each time I told of the tiny pigmy possum falling from a rafter onto my shoulder, scrambling into my long windblown hair, curling its sticky tail around a tendril and nesting there for two days. The small warmth of that hapless creature was like a second heart beating, the children fed it on honey water from a dropper until we located its mother. She came shyly closer to us across the rafter to retrieve her babe from foster care.

Silence fell after the telling of tales.

The coals glowed in the fire; we passed the talking stick, passed it on.

I remembered threading my way through tall grass along the dusty track on my land on the north of the island. It was the best time of day, soon after sunrise. I noticed a familiar old wombat approaching. I stopped stone-still as he sniffed the air, he moved gingerly towards me, his fat shiny nose upturned as I stood silent and breathing so slowly I might have dropped to the track for lack of air. He approached warily, encountered my old worn boot, explored up onto my rainbow sock and moved his attention to my bare leg. Oh! The wet surface of his nose was a sweet strawberry kiss. It travelled the height of my shin, rested there, oh, oh! His doleful eyes gazed up at me and he ambled off, his wide rump swinging from side to side like a weighted pendulum. A moment of true communion, an island moment, isolated as we were on the white ribbon of the track. The making of legends in these anecdotes, the making of myth.

. . .

One thing leads to another, one story chains itself to my heart and then it flies out like a kestrel thread ready to knit itself into a cloud pattern. I conjure up images of islands floating on shimmering horizons, mystical islands and mythical islands. How I long for the ineffable comfort and isolation a remote island offers as I gaze at the floating mass just hanging there on the edge. Words like islands, words like sand.

Words like grandmother.

Madi. A universal grandmother. Maddelina di Castello lived in the castle on the outcrop of land above the Piazza Garibaldi in a tiny village at the Gulf of the Poets in Italy. I paid homage to her each time I visited that sacred place. She was the muse of a poet, a resistance worker during the war, a keeper of a back packer accommodation, Ostello della Gioventu, taking over that role in 1949, the year I was born. Here she hid people away to escape possible imprisonment or death.

Surely Madi would gaze out, as I did decades later, at the island Palmaria opposite? It was only a short ride in a fishing boat to reach its shores. How often did she visit that tiny island I wonder? Did she escape there to find peace in the time of unrest and political mayhem? Was she too a lover of flowery frocks, honey, apricots and birdsong?

Isolate. Isola. Island. To be an island to oneself, no man is an island, no woman either, words igniting flashpoints of illuminated manuscripts, candle flames of monks in tiny vessels made from goatskins, codices forever etched on granite, stories growing in groves, forests of bones and roots of blood.

The ghost of Maddelina di Castello is said to haunt the castle; was it her voice I heard urging me on and up the steps and down into the vaults of underground escape routes? I finger the periwinkle of words in my pocket, thinking about war now, whispered stories hidden from children with big ears, children who yearned to know the dark secrets.

The small grandmother from the island down south was born in the upstairs room on the left of the stairs in the old red brick house. It nestled behind the pine trees on the point looking across to Tinderbox. Gwen grew up with two sisters in that house by the sea. Cousins lived on the island, further south. They took turns to deliver the mail, riding side saddle along dusty winding tracks through the whispering she oaks along the coast.

Gwen married Norman when she was young, when her black hair fell to her waist and her legs were strong from walking over the hills and far away. They went with brave hearts and true to live in the small white house overlooking the bay on the east coast of North Bruny. The maker of that house chose a perfect spot to build; Betsy Island was in full view, the land sloped down to the rocky shore and a garden was wrestled from the poor soil.

Walnut and mulberry trees provided shade in the garden, dark berries hanging like lanterns delighted the children as they clambered into the branches, returning stained and grinning like demons with red lips. From the hall a stairway led to the rooms above, one room faced north, the other south. Windows like eyes closing on dusk, opening to bright striated dawns. The kitchen was on the west side, where Gwen cooked local fare for her growing family and baked the daily bread in a baker's oven.

Norman's family were flour millers. The first flour mill in Hobart was established by one of his ancestors. Her flour, tea and assorted dry goods were stored in a large cellar underneath the kitchen floor. She bore six children to Norman.

He died young and Nanna went to live in a larger house on the shore of the Derwent in Lindisfarne. On summer evenings she would sit on the porch of the white, wooden house remembering her mother gazing out to sea, resting back on the settle on long summer evenings on the wide porch of the red brick house at Dennes Point. Two children were buried out there on the point, lost to diphtheria in the days when a boat was the only means of transport across to the mainland.

. . .

There were so many gaps now in her remembered stories, the pear tree resurfaced from somewhere far away as she sat in the shade and she remembered the apricot tree and the jam cooling in jars.

Words like jars. Words like summer. Like apricots.

The words were golden and smelled of honey. She fingered the lace of the doily she was making and the humming sound of the bees took her back to another life and she thought about the grass trees, the Xanthorrhoea trees of her childhood, the stories of the original inhabitants of the island, the first people who used the medicine from the trees, the sap for spear making and as a glue in repairing water containers. Later, it was used as a resin in making varnish and as a waterproofing agent in protecting boxes of food sent to soldiers in New Guinea in the war.

Her thoughts melted like the honeyed sap and flowed down the wooden hook and into the foam she was tatting on the pristine white sands of the doily on her lap. She remembered her lost husband Norman, his sister Leila who was presumed drowned when returning from Italy just after the war, his brave lost sister who set up a hospice for wounded soldiers in Brindisi on the coast, his lost sister whose lonely bones are thought to mingle with the seaweed and stones at the bottom of the straits between Australia and New Guinea. The hook trembles in her veined stiff hands, the circle of lace grows, large enough to hold her long sparkling life, small enough to tuck into her pocket.

My grandmother was a tiny woman. I hardly knew her and her absence created a gap to fill with other grandmothers. Women like Madi, painterly desert women like Emily, island women like Doris and embroiderers like Vanda. So many absences, lack of presences. My maternal grandmother died when my mother was a teenager, and my own mother went under the wheels of a speeding car when I was only a few years older, before children came along.

Gaps in the arsenal of my familial memories, one by one they were filled and life became rich, overloaded with stories stretching way across the seas and across land masses, through wars and famines, into deserts and reservations.

Grandmothers. So often the moral compass of families rests in the hands of ageing women. I sought them out, grateful for the emptiness, a sky without stars, a blank canvas. A grandmother myself now, I take up the needle and thread and mark wordy moments on cloth.

Words like pears, like apricots, like islands and dirt tracks and shearwaters; words like nautilus; words like horizon and words like nets.

Netted and caught fast in the fraying spider web of my reveries, my grandmothers' memories, and their grandmothers' memories. The making of myths.

I tie my favourite orange and turquoise apron around me; it is exactly the colours of the lichen on granite on the island and the bright sea surrounding it — a shouting metallic orange, turquoise like the marbles in the jar on my dresser.

I put the kettle on for tea and go to the garden to gather windfall apples, plums and peaches for jam. I see black shadows dancing across the sandstone pavers, look skyward, with gratitude, as the cries of the black cockies herald rain.

ROD FRANCISCO is an amateur writer who has written on and off for many years and has the avid collection folders and journals of half-finished works and ideas. Writing more for personal enjoyment than anything else, Rod has engaged in writing in a range of different styles in poetry, short stories and scripts; some of which have been published and longlisted. He lives on a secluded acreage block nestled amongst the rainforest, a short drive out of Mackay in central Queensland. He makes a living as an executive in human resources.

The fire is out

ROD FRANCISCO

The young man walked slowly from the emergency services vehicle, up to the ruins of the home. More than just a house, most certainly a home, not one he had lived in though. As he surveyed the charred and blackened remains, he unexpectedly saw two fireproof steel boxes neatly placed, rather ironically, next to the fireplace. A weatherproof tin of sorts sat askew on top, although he suspected that it would have been much more neatly positioned before the fire. Both were scorched from the fire, but he knew that they would have been purposely chosen to withstand the heat and flames.

He reached down and picked up the tin. It was warm to touch which was more from the sun than the fire that had raged through and razed this home to nothing more than burnt, twisted and broken images. Gently and with trepidation he twisted the lid which initially resisted, then slowly gave way to an inquisitive pair of hands. He wiped his blackened hands on his jeans before reaching in to lift out the folded pieces of paper that were browned from the heat but relatively untouched.

As he unfolded the papers, he immediately recognised the hand-writing ... not that he had expected otherwise ...

If you are reading this, the fire must be out. That is a good thing and I am glad that is so.

My fire is also out.

I'm burnt, done.

. . .

The Channel Eight news reporter blinked into the sun during an update to the camera:

"The emergency services coordinator has stated that the Blanchard Island bridge is now closed to all non-essential traffic. Evacuations may commence in the morning depending upon wind directions. It was also stated that not all residents were accounted for and that concerns were held for residents located further up the island's valley."

The fire had started in an old regrowth zone at the bottom of the valley, well away from the main residential area on the coast strip astride the Blanchard River. Naming conventions had not been a big focus for the island as it had only one river and one valley, a narrow valley shaped like a squashed horseshoe. There had been extensive logging of the island for its rare eucalyptus type – the rainbow gum – that was not found anywhere else on the mainland and no longer on the island. The loggers had ripped out every specimen and the regrowth had been a wild mix of other gums that called the island home. Every here and there, a reminder of the rainbow gum could be seen on different heritage listed parts of the residential area, but the loggers had left nothing behind. They had been there for a good time, not a long time.

With only gentle sea breezes to fan the fire, it had been left to burn under an "advice" warning that one morning quickly escalated to a "watch and act" when the brutally strong winds crashed through an otherwise calm and unremarkable dawn. At that point, emergency sirens wailed up the valley with heartfelt sincerity and grimness. Unpredictably, the fire closed the valley access road almost immediately, which caused a somewhat comical parade of farm and off-road vehicles as they traversed down the valley via series of paddock gates and farm trails all whilst trying to avoid spot fires and flying embers.

One gate had remained closed and locked. No-one had tried to come down through it.

. . .

I can hear the sirens and smell the smoke. The fire is distant, but my decisions are close. Undoubtedly there will be those holding great concerns and seeking an opportunity to come to my aid. Never would I consider that I needed saving although I suspect that is probably not an opinion that is shared. The one thing I do not want is for anyone to do anything foolish and risk their life for mine. That happened once before and I have lived with that regret ever since. There is nothing I can do about that and it has torn at my soul every day since; not a waking moment goes by without wishing I could undo that fateful moment. Our country recognised that act as the highest level of courage, but I lacked the courage to face the family left behind. That same lack of courage has led me to these decisions. I can no longer face those who remain, it simply does not work for me anymore. It is hard to see clearly when your eyes are filled with emotion that rages violently, mixing anger and despair into a volatile combination of deep sadness and aggression.

Sadly, I imagine that you will have travelled across the travesty that is the bridge that was built to connect this island to the rest of the world. A bridge that never needed to be built, a bridge that took away my isolation from a world that had gone wrong; that had done nothing but create continued sadness. People who know me though would say that I burnt my bridges well before that bridge was ever built and that may be true. I retreated from the world, from the people in it, from the tragedy that society seemed to think it needed to inflict on itself at frequent and regular intervals. I withdrew to my island to remove myself from society's woes and ill tidings, and society from mine. There is nothing pretty left in life and certainly not in me. I cannot fathom how ugly society has got; to call it civilisation would be an overstatement of the prefix 'civil' in any context. I hope you understand that I never meant to burn you. In an effort to shield you from the fiery maelstrom that I had become you were pushed away to a safe distance, beyond my emotional firebreak, away from my anger driven spot fires.

My life had become unpleasant. I had seen the horror of what people can do in the name of ideologically driven hatred; I would see it again at night in broken dreams. It sickened me deep into my soul and often I would sit alone in the dark with wine and music so to drown it out. It was never successful because every dawn would bring it all flooding back with the rays of the new day. I can never remove the memory of retching so deep and hard that I wished my own insides would spill out onto the dirty and dusty ground, and that I could then fall into a deep unconsciousness from which I would never need to wake. So deep was that wish, that I almost treasured the taste of bile in my throat as punishment for not being stronger when it counted.

You have seen some of the ugliness of my life although you always hoped for that silver lining, that sliver of hope that one day I could see some hope in the world. Sadly, I always knew that day would never come but I could never bring myself to tell you. Time and time again I told myself that I owed this to you so I hope that in writing this letter, you appreciate that I never wanted to say goodbye to anything but then spent an eternity wishing I could farewell the grim, the sad, the hurt, the anger and the ugly. You must understand that this self-loathing is not about anything between me and you; it is between me and the man I once was, that I left behind in the dusty hills of vengeance and hate.

I was enjoying my ocean of isolation and then society drifted its smoke and haze over me, adding to my gloom but not my despair. Having done society's bidding, I though it owed me an opportunity to be alone in my reflections. Instead it demanded I get up again and again, until I no longer cared whether I got up or where I fell. So, I have chosen to not get up one more time and I am quite content with that. Whilst unexpected in timing, this is the moment that I have deeply and covertly desired. I know I never communicated this as I knew you would want to save me in some way. Coughing your way through the haze that is enveloping me, the smoke adding to the tears in your eyes … no thank you. That is not pain you need to endure.

Sitting here, I can feel the heat from the fire…I can hear the roaring crackling of trees bursting with light as the flames explode their inner oils … I can smell the burning of the fuel laden bush floor.

As I write, I can tell that I am enveloped by fire in my safe space but still surrounded by ocean. You know who I am and yet you regret that I became an emotional island. Having been isolated for a long time it will be sad for you to find me and my things like this. Do not despair at the destruction the fire has caused to my belongings or what the world has caused to me; just be content that you have had a chance to read this and sift through those things that I considered most treasured. There are no secrets in there, no sudden revelations, no sinister secrets that are left unexplained. There are only memories, both good and bad; of family and friends, both near and far; of brothers in arms, both past and present but also still lost. Hopefully you will realise that I was not lost, once I had found myself in this place. I appreciate that you may have felt that you lost me when I came here but I was lost to everyone a long time before that. I needed to find myself.

As I withdrew across the empty space that the ocean provided, I always knew that society and its ill ways would eventually catch up to me. As much as I may have wanted to, there was nowhere to run to, and no time left to run. You would have argued that I could have run to you and been safe. As much as I would have liked to believe that, I fear that I would never have been safe and would have simply endangered you and your life unnecessarily. You owed me nothing, something I cannot say about myself for you. I owe you everything and can only leave you this letter and what is in those boxes.

In an effort to reflect and maybe restore, I would sit in the small mountain pool and watch the river waters run fast and deep down the valley with the summer rains. On a clear day, early in the season, you could see the plume of the summer rains flushing out to sea, like an emotional cleansing. As much as I tried though, I never felt clean. I meditated on the smooth rocks, allowing the sun to radiate me with its warmth and life and simply blocked myself out into the nature surrounding me. Sadly, on too many occasions, something dark would always knock me back into reality and break my disconnection. I learned to block out even the most extremes of the screaming and crying but it never truly went away.

. . .

The emergency evacuation sirens screamed at the valley. Almost pleading one final time for evacuation.

"Emergency services have confirmed that there is only one resident unaccounted for. They have also confirmed that there is no ability to reach him and hope that he has not gambled on being able to defend against this fire."

. . .

The piercing sound of the sirens has jolted me. Sorry, I had paused for a moment, lost in my boxed memories for a moment there. The screaming sirens reminded me of those who had pleaded for their lives as good men did bad things in the name of virtuous ideology. As with everything, there are always sounds, smells and scenes that can never be eradicated from your mind no matter how hard you try. I was having one of those occasions and I was paused in that moment, wondering how to change what was about to occur. Not a matter of reflection but an earnest desire to go back and undo the bad.

Everything is in these two boxes which you can open with the keys that were in this tin. Whilst not quite how I expected it would end, I always kept these in fireproof boxes just in case I did not get a chance to prepare. Just like those days in hot dusty places in foreign countries where no amount of preparation was enough for what we encountered. I came here to this island to get away from it all, from everything whilst knowing you desperately wanted to find me, to reach out and ask, to talk. I just couldn't do that ... I was too broken. I could never tell you stories you should never have to hear. You did not deserve the pain and anguish of those stories, best you be left with my loss this time, once only, as opposed to the many times I have been lost *"over there"*, as some say, knowing I never fully *"came back"*.

I know you have a love of music and it has probably helped with your healing, so I guess it's appropriate to close with a couple of song references for you. Kenny Rogers once wrote *"And every hand's a loser. And the best that you can hope for is to die in your sleep"* but I am not a gambler and there will be no more sleep. I have taken my risks and gambled a few things but there was never time to sleep, least of all now. There is little time now for rest and there is nothing left to gamble. I have made my decisions. Not every hand is a loser either, some are just crappy hands that get dealt when the stakes are highest. This is no crappy hand, but it is the highest of stakes — one last hand. There is also a Simon and Garfunkel song too, with the lines *"I am a rock. I am an island. And rock feels no pain. And an island never cries."* I always thought of myself as a rock and so desperately wanted to be an island; but I have felt immeasurable pain and have cried on the inside, deeply. I hope these help you understand who I was.

The Channel Eight news reporter struggled in the blustery and smoky conditions …

"Authorities have confirmed that the Blanchard Island fire has been contained and that recovery efforts are now underway. Sadly, they have also confirmed that they have found the body of the missing man. It was reported that the man was suspected of being trapped in his remote home at the top end of the main valley. Locals report that the man had generally kept to himself and had not often mixed with other island residents, although that he had been quite pleasant and respectful when in town. The local veterans' group has confirmed that the man was a former special forces soldier who had sought solitude away from a world that had left him broken and sad. It was well known that he had considered his home an island, a refuge from the world outside. A world away from tragedy that, sadly, has once again befallen him for one last time."

. . .

The young man stopped reading and just stood there as tears welled in eyes. His father had been gone emotionally for many years. Now he was simply gone. Burnt like the home he had retreated to, leaving memories in the charred debris of life.

BEVERLEY LELLO lives with her husband on a bush block on the edge of Yackandandah in north-east Victoria. She was once an English and Literature teacher and now retirement has given her the opportunity to pursue two of her passions, writing and travelling. Her travels are often an inspiration for her stories. Her short stories have been published in Country Style, *page seventeen, fourW,* Award Winning Australian Writing *and several Stringybark Publishing and Margaret River Press anthologies. Beverley also encourages others to write by conducting writers' workshops in her area. She formed the Yackandandah Writers Group three years ago and many of the members have entered, and won, short story competitions. Beverley has published two collections of short stories,* Tailwind *and* Borrowed Spaces. *See more on her website, beverleylello.com.*

Walk, don't run

BEVERLEY LELLO

When I awoke in the half-formed light of dawn, I struggled to remember where I was. I rolled over and saw my father's sleeping bag, a deflated hump. *Where was he?* There was no point trying to go back to sleep. Once the worry surfaced it was like pushing that sleeping bag into its sack, a puffed edge always poking out. I felt around in the dark space for my pile jacket and beanie, unzipped the door of the tent and pulled on my boots, still damp from wading the icy river the evening before. I followed the path down to the edge of the lake. A gauzy membrane of mist obscured the hills, the sky and the steely water of the lake — air, water and sky floating as one.

My father, Dougal, was crouched on the pebbly beach, his gaze fixed on the lake. The water nudged the pebbles, a gentle lapping.

"It's cold, Dad."

"I couldn't sleep."

"It's not even light yet."

"The night was long enough."

I knew he'd been restless. The ground was uneven; it was difficult to get comfortable. "Are you still taking the pills?"

"Threw them away."

He was blocking me. Hard to be sympathetic when he puts the wall up. "They're supposed to help." Frustration made my voice ragged.

"Help me do what?" He picked up a small stone and stood up.

"I don't know. Calm you. Give you some time out."

"Nick, has it occurred to you I might not want time out?"

"Sorry, I'm putting it wrong … maybe you've got to have some time when you don't think about her."

He considered the stone in his hand. A flick of his wrist and it bounced across the smooth surface of the lake. Five skips before it sank. I remembered him teaching me how to choose the best stone for skipping, showing me the technique with the wrist, praising me when I managed three in a row. "Her? Your mother, you mean?"

"Of course. Sorry. Mum."

"Stop saying sorry."

"You're not making it easy."

"Should I be?"

In fact, I thought, *you're making it bloody difficult. She was my mother.* I knew it wasn't the same though. My father had lost the person who was always by his side: friend, companion, lover. He was 70, she'd been 68; they'd had two decades of plans. I wanted him to think there was still good things to come, that it wasn't all behind him. My kids, his grand-kids, holidays, travelling, old friends, new people to meet.

"Dad, it's been six months."

"So, I should be over it then?"

"She's not coming back."

"I know that, but it doesn't mean I don't wish she was right here now standing next to me looking at the mist on the lake. She'd have her sketch book open drawing the skeleton of that tree, the rocks sticking out of the water."

"It's a beautiful place. That's why we're here now. You and me." And it was. That view yesterday when we crossed the ridge. We'd stopped. Marvelled. We'd shared that. Now I realised he was wishing it was my mother standing next to him. *I'm wasting my time,* I thought. *All he wants to do is wallow in his misery.* I decided on silence, but he was ratchetting up, injecting some bitterness into the conversation.

"Father and son."

"Dad, I can't be mum. I can't fill that hole."

"Nope." He paused. I waited. His tone softened as he stooped again. "I know you're trying to help, Nick." This time he tossed a handful of pebbles into the water, a scattershot disturbance on the surface then all was still again.

"It was probably a mistake to do this hike. We should have gone somewhere new."

"I've tried that," he said. "Three months in the Outback with the dog for company. It was no different. I saw a tree bent in the wind and thought, Grace would've wanted to sketch that. An art gallery. Grace would've had me in the door. New place, old place. I want her to be with me."

"What can I do?"

"You're doing it."

"It doesn't feel like I'm helping."

"Trust me, it would be worse if I didn't have you. And Lucy. And the twins."

"What next?"

"Breakfast. Coffee. Let's get walking. It's a six-hour hike today."

. . .

I didn't want to feel responsible for my father's happiness. When my mother was diagnosed, we all seemed to have a purpose. Trips to hospital then home again, adjusting to care rosters, another round of chemo followed by a few weeks of comparative calm. Dougal embraced it, created a Facebook page – not to give progress reports, but to advance his campaign for voluntary euthanasia in Queensland. Mum became his cause as well as his life. We were all swept along, busy trying to make her final weeks bearable, not really believing that the end would eventually come. Our twins, Violet and Oliver, were in their first year of school. We tried to establish a balance between keeping things normal for them and preparing them for the fact that Grandma wouldn't be there for very much longer. Their Grandma Grace, storyteller, lover of messy painting projects, breaker of food rules.

When the inevitable happened, Dougal used Facebook to announce it, took a deep breath and weathered the memorial service and the scattering of her ashes in the rainforest. He then loaded the other love of his life, his much travelled Landcruiser, with his camping gear and their grieving dog and drove west. I was left waving my hand forlornly as the vehicle, Dad and the dog disappeared around the corner of our suburban street.

"Why's Grandpa going away?" Violet asked. "He needs to stay here so he won't be lonely without Grandma."

I tried to be reassuring. "Sometimes when you lose a person you love you want to be by yourself for awhile. To think about them. He'll miss us. He'll come back when he's ready."

"I hope he's ready very soon because he said he'd build us a cubby."

I picked her up and buried my face in her hair. She smelled of vanilla and I couldn't conceive of a world without her and Oliver and Lucy.

During their long and crazy marriage, Dougal and Grace had loved long distance walking, packs on their backs, dehydrated food, campsites on windswept ridges, tiring trudges across grassy plains, the more remote the better. As a child, I'd been kitted out with smaller versions of packs, sleeping bags, boots. Every holiday we went hiking, no exceptions. Our family was a team. I wanted to experience this connection again so, when he returned from his three months in the desert, I suggested we walk the Overland Track in Tasmania. He hesitated but agreed.

. . .

So here we were on the third day of our hike, the early morning scene at Lake Windermere behind us, a day's walking ahead. I was getting into my stride, concentrating on the back of my father's legs; the still strong calf muscles, the dark hairs, the thick socks bunched around the top of his battered walking boots. We were hiking through an area of pandanus when Dad said, "Can you remember the time we walked this track in autumn. You were only ten, I think. It snowed during the night and when you stepped outside the hut you said, 'It's like in Narnia.'" As soon as he said Narnia, I could feel the warmth of Mum's body as I snuggled up to her on the couch, hear her reading *The Lion, the Witch and the Wardrobe*.

My throat constricted. "The snow that morning, it was my fantasy come true," I managed to say. "On the leaves, the branches and those weird pineapple plants …"

"Pandanus."

"Pandanus. How crazy was that, snow and pineapples. Anyway, Narnia. I remember it felt like I'd opened the wardrobe door, pushed the coats aside and stepped into wonderland." I paused. "I loved it when Mum read me that book."

The boots stumbled and recovered. We walked on in silence. It felt good to be negotiating the rough track, slogging through the mud, pounding the boardwalk sections built to protect the fragile ground. I could feel the weight of the pack on my back, the slight rubbing on my heel that I hoped wouldn't form into a blister, thinking, as I walked, how easily I'd used the "Mum" word.

That evening, we pitched the tent away from Pelion Hut on an area of tufty grass. An hour earlier, before we'd reached the designated campsite, a young couple had loped up behind and passed with a friendly greeting in heavily accented English. She was in her twenties, tall and slim. He was older, his face rugged. I watched them disappear around a bend in the track. Were they reminding Dad of his hiking days with Mum, striding along tracks in distant countries, passing locals and surprising them with their funny accents? Dad had been silent since the Narnia conversation so I hadn't asked. I was learning to recognise the moments when he welcomed me onto his island.

When we stumbled into the camping area, the couple had already pitched their tent and were huddled over a stove. They acknowledged us with a wave. My bare legs were grimed with mud; sweat had dried on my back where the pack clung. According to the map, Pelion Falls was another ten minutes' walk upstream.

"A dip would be nice," I said.

Dad followed, reluctantly.

The falls cascaded over a ledge into a dark pool below. I knew the water would be very cold but, "I'm going in," I said, sliding off a smooth rock. It was the kind of swimming where you had to keep moving; a moment when the sharp sting of the water sucked the breath out of you, a quick plunge before surfacing, skin shuddering with the smack of cold air, a few strokes to the falls, another duck dive. When

I surfaced again, Dad was there next to me, yipping and yelling like a kid, plunging back under and surfacing again like a seal, the water streaming off his grey beard.

We clambered onto the rocks at the edge of the falls, our skin tingling. Sat in companionable silence, listening to the chatter of birds as they roosted. Aware that the light was dimming. Reluctant to break the spell.

"I'll start the meal," he said, slipping his clothes back on and sliding his feet into his boots.

I lingered watching the insects make concentric circles on the smooth surface of the pool, succeeded in losing myself in the moment. When I did return to the camp, the couple were sitting with Dad on a log. As I approached, I caught the end of a familiar story "… and so we wound up spending the night on a ledge." His face was animated by the memory – the story of his youthful hiking days with his favourite companion, my mother. A sunny weather system had settled on his face. "We were never really in danger," he continued. "Bloody uncomfortable though." I watched, detached from the scene. As he finished the story, the light in his eyes dulled, a cloud obscured the sun. But the woman – later I learnt her name was Marina – must have already been told the story of the absent wife. She blew the cloud away when she said, "It's so nice to share a scary experience with someone. I think for you the night was very cold, but the memory is very warm." I wished they were my words.

I approached the group, rolling my eyes. Dad knew what I thought of his near-death campfire stories. The grin he offered me had the warmth of a shot of whiskey on an empty stomach.

The couple drifted away to finish their meal and we settled down to eat ours.

"I'm off for a wander," Dad said, after rinsing our empty plates and cutlery.

"Just a sec. I'll grab my parka. It's getting cold."

"Alone. I'm having a bit of a wander, that's all."

"Oh, okay … sure."

"I won't get lost."

"Of course, you won't. I was only thinking that—"

"You are helping, Nick."

I felt a sting of tears, wanted to hug him but he'd turned away and headed towards the stand of trees and the start of the track we'd follow the next day. He was like a large fish hooked on the end of a line, allowing himself to be reeled in then pulling against the force, struggling to stay independent. This father was difficult to deal with, distant and remote, yet there had been that conversation earlier — the Narnia stuff — the swim, the grin when he knew I was laughing at his story.

I pushed my half-empty pack against a rock and leant back. The light was almost gone leaving the silhouette of the tree canopy etched against the sky. I was tired after a day's hard hiking, let my mind drift onto mundane things, faded into sleep.

When he returned, he poked me in the ribs. "Hey, Nick, you might be more comfortable in your sleeping bag."

. . .

On our fourth day, we walked in the morning, dropped our packs at a saddle, Pelion Gap, and headed off on a side trip to the summit of Mt Ossa. The sky was clear as we made the steady upward ascent to a steep, boulder-strewn gully and the route to the summit. The way was well marked with cairns and involved some scrambling and stepping across a few exposed sections. Eventually, we were above the gully and wandering across an area of tarns to the summit. From there you could see halfway across Tasmania.

"You could lose your soul in such a place," Dad said, as we sat like an audience at a concert pointing out landmarks, tracing the way we'd come from the north.

Cloud was rolling in from the west as we began our descent, and thickened as we negotiated the boulders above the gully.

We batted instructions to each other. "I think we should go towards the left."

"It looks blocked to me."

"Have you seen a cairn?"

"I'll go ahead," Dad said. "I'm pretty sure it's this way."

The mist swirled and parted before gathering in a thickness that made it difficult for me to see where to put my boot next. I slid it across the surface of the rock searching for a solid footing so that I could move down. Another parting of the curtain and I glimpsed the top of my father's head. Grey hair, grey rock, grey mist but I couldn't see the way he'd taken.

I called out. "Don't get too far ahead. I can't see anything." My voice sounded muffled, sucked up by the fog. Had he heard? Was I going the right way? I slid down a bit further and settled my boot onto a precarious foothold.

My fingers, scraping across the cold rock, had become numb. "Dad, where are you?" I made another cautious move down. My heavy boot slipped and sent a rush of loose rock tumbling. I visualised myself plummeting after it, twisting and somersaulting before coming to rest in a spreadeagled tangle of broken bones somewhere far below. I pulled myself closer to the rock face and tried to conjure a different image — eating a hot meal at the next campsite, crawling into a warm sleeping bag — anything but the plunge over the side.

"You okay? Glad it was only a rock and not you nearly knocking me over." Dad's voice floated up from below; so far away.

I tried to answer. Words were pasted in my mouth. I wanted to say, "Just a sec, I'm not feeling very balanced." I imagined my voice making light of the fact I was frozen onto the rock face, clutching onto a hold that threatened to give way at any minute. I couldn't go up. Or down. Thoughts drained away. I was alone with my fear.

...

He climbed back up. Calmed me with words. Coaxed me into movement by offering the image of Lucy and the twins running towards me when I arrived back in Melbourne. The soft gentle caress of his words helped me feel their hugs and, eventually, spurred me into making that first awkward move. It wasn't difficult.

Several metres below, a narrow ledge offered a resting place. "You've never liked heights," Dad said, as I slumped down next to him.

We sat, two roosting pigeons, feeling the temperature drop as the mist continued to swirl in dense billowy curtains, but parting and offering reassuring glimpses of the base of the gully and the distant plains below.

Dad manoeuvred his daypack so that it formed a bench between us and unzipped the top pocket. "I've been saving this," he said, pulling out a squashed Cherry Ripe bar and tearing back the red and silver paper. He broke it in two and handed me half.

I sank my teeth into the cloying sweetness. My father's gaze was fixed, not on me, but looking out as if he could see through the mist and what lay beyond. I took another bite, tried to swallow as I said, "Is this our trapped-on-a-ledge-we-could-die moment?" I tried to make my tone light and jokey, but my words were clogged with chocolate and the fear that I might be trampling on a memory, possibly a sacred one. I swallowed again and managed, "Am I going to be boring my kids stupid with this story in the years to come?"

When he finally turned his head and looked at me, he said, "I hope so, I really hope so."

RI QUIN is a writer living and working from her home in regional Queensland. Her work is inspired by outback landscapes and a love of solitude.

Waiting for dolphins

RI QUIN

I flounder in waves that crash and break around me. I tumble with them, feel the rush of water past my ears, the grit of sand against my skin and I can do nothing but give myself over to the force of the ocean. No strength is great enough to tame it, no voice loud enough to silence it. This thing is bigger and more enigmatic than anything. All I can do is let it buffet me about so I lose all sense of who I am, and where I am. Let it dash my head against the sand, fill my mouth with gritty, salty wave and my eyes with sand and foam.

When I drag myself from the waves I feel my head spin and the long white beach tilts and swims before my eyes. The sand is warm, the sun hot on slick wet skin and I lie down and stare into the blue of the sky. I'm alone on this beach, gulls flying between me and the blue sky. They squawk and glide on air currents and disturb a silence that is not a silence at all. More a stillness. The sound of crashing waves making silence impossible, but stillness plausible. There's anonymity to lying alongside the crashing of waves and the contrasting stillness of the long, white beach.

I recover from my dunking and realise the danger. I imagine my body, thrashed by waves and hurled back out onto the beach, to be found a week from now by a solitary fisherman striding along the shore. My mother would be horrified by my behaviour. *Irresponsible and selfish* she would say. *You don't give a thought to how I would feel if you died on some lonesome beach on the other side of the world,* she'd say. And she would be right. I don't care. But I would give some thought to how I would feel about checking out of life in that particular way. A week ago I wouldn't have minded. A week ago checking out had been a viable option.

"This is Ella. Her divorce came through last week." That was my mother, standing beside the barbeque, red wine in hand, her second or third, definitely not her last. *"You'd think she'd be pleased. It's what she wanted."* She put her hand on the man's arm, Harry or Joseph, I can't remember which. My sister's latest boyfriend. *"Couldn't make it work you know. The sweetest man in the world and she couldn't make it work."* Harry/Joseph wanted to escape. I could see it in his eyes. I gave him a tight smile of encouragement and left them for the drinks fridge. That sweetest man in the world who'd captured me in some bizarre alternate world that resembled re-runs of the Brady Bunch. I could never play the part of the little wife, cooking and cleaning. Hosting dinner parties. But he broke my heart all the same. Apparently men in the 60s always had affairs with their secretaries. Such a cliché. I got out, but not unscathed. Without the affair I might have stayed, and if I'd stayed I would have been miserable. Thanks Sandy with the swishy blond hair and sing-song voice. I die in the waves on a deserted beach with the voice of Sandy in my head.

...

The nightclub is down the road from the hostel. I avoid it. The place has a dynamic energy, a beast with a life of its own. Instead I sit on the balcony overlooking the bay, drink wine, listening to voices fade in and out. So young, these people I share a small section of my life with. They are unconcerned by the things that consume me. I seek their simplicity, but can't seem to find it. So many things in my head. A life lived. What does that mean?

"You should take your opportunities." That's my mother again. She doesn't mean *my* opportunities. She means the ones she considers important. Travel to Europe on a 24-day bus tour, marry the man, ignore minor indiscretions, start a family. She doesn't mean scream at the man, go through with the divorce, take the job with the international engineering firm, travel to some out-of-the-way place on a budget to find myself. My mother and I have very different opinions when it comes to recognising and taking opportunities.

The sound of the night club, music thumping. It's the bass notes that reach furthest out into the night, pulsing and beating the air, a call to action, an invitation to give up the seat overlooking the bay, give up the glass of wine and follow the Pied Piper. Night after night it's the background sound, and then it's not. It becomes the main feature to influence the night. They wear me down, those young, energetic, nocturnal creatures who have been sharing this life of mine for the past two weeks. They wear me down and I agree to go with them to the nightclub.

My body pulses with the music. It starts at the top of my head, entering my system through the nerves in my brain and spreading out through my arms and my fingers, controlling the movement of my legs and the pounding of my feet. I jump and scream and cover my face with my hands. The light strobes across the pulsing herd. And with the music the alcohol runs through my veins and out into the extremities of who I am. I can't control what it does to me. Then there is something else. At the edge of my mind I see a white tablet in the palm of my hand. A smiling face, the nod of a head. Enough encouragement for me. Anything is possible.

We drive through thick rainforest along a road that is a tunnel and only the headlights keep us grounded to the earth. They've dragged me after them, into the back of the jeep. They sing and stand up to scream at the passing night. I see myself join them. I'm standing back watching, yet at the same time, leaning forward adding my breath to the wind.

The shack on the edge of the sand, between beach and forest, is lit by candles and the lights from the jeep. Music thumps out of the car stereo. They dance like shadows and laugh and drink and dance some more. So young. They are so young and I drift away from them out past the light.

The sky is beginning to lighten when I hear them calling. I have no time for them. I close my eyes and sleep. Sleep. Sleep. Sinking down into it, so deep, so luxurious. There's no place in my dreams for the young things calling my name.

When I wake the sun is higher and I'm alone. Completely alone. I'm me again. A little battered, but I know myself. I don't recognise the person who came here in the middle of the night. My head aches in a way it's never ached before and I am alone. I am surrounded by forest, green, verdant growth. A thickness that crowds in, leaving no air between it, no sky visible above it. How am I here in this jungle on my own?

Through the fog in my head I hear her. *You always get yourself into these predicaments.* My mother would say that if I had a phone and I could call her. Always? She'd say that and I know I've never been alone in a forest before, not knowing where I am or how to get myself out. That's never happened before. *I'm always the one who has to get you out of these scrapes.* Always? She's never rescued my from a thick tropical jungle, never found me when I was alone and lost.

. . .

The sight of the shack is a relief, as if finding it somehow makes things better. It's familiar, though I have no claim to it other than some vague memory. But it's a point of anchorage. A place to start, and a place to end if all other paths lead nowhere. There are bottles strewn around, an untidy pile of wrappers from a take-away store. I don't remember food. They flap around and a breeze moves them in procession towards the beach. I clean up. I'm not generally a tidy person, but this scarred scene is incongruous between the sea and the forest. I imagine hamburger wrappers dancing in waves and slapped in a soggy mess onto the beach. I imagine broken glass hidden and waiting to pierce flesh, under a swathe of leaf litter. I tidy up because I imagine things and because I can't think of anything else to do.

Two lines of tyre track lead off along the sandy road. It makes sense to follow them. I don't know how far I'll have to walk, and don't know which direction to take if there's a choice up ahead. It makes sense to get started, but instead, I walk along the beach. The tyre tracks and sandy road can wait a little. I've never been lost like this before. It frightens me, but I want to investigate that feeling of fear for just a little while.

The beach ends in a rocky headland and I climb over sharp rocks, past tidal rock pools and higher up to find a view of the ocean and the feeling of sea breeze strengthening to gusty billows of air. There's a foot track. I follow it and find a sheltered area at the edge of a rocky cliff that plummets down directly into the skirt of white foam and churning blue ocean.

I don't see her at first. She's tucked in beside a boulder, small, like a child. I recognise her from the hostel. She's always off to the side, reading, writing or drawing in a small thick book. Her hair is jet black, blue-black, and here on the cliff she has pulled it back and covered it with a scarf. Beside her, on a flattened indent in the rock, is a camera with a telephoto lens. She sits beside the camera with her hand resting near it, her eyes searching the ocean.

"Hello." This is a strange place for the sound of voices.

She turns, but seems reluctant to take her eyes off the ocean. The only acknowledgement I receive is a nod. She returns to her searching.

I take this encouragement and move forward, lower myself onto the wild grassy patch of stony ground a little way from the cliff and a little way from her. Here in the loneliness I seek her companionship when I have never done so before.

"You're the one from the hostel. I recognise you."

She nods again but doesn't take the time to look at me.

"I'm lost," I say and am surprised that there are tears. I've been holding my fear in check and finding her has given me more relief than I expected. "I don't know how to get back."

"They say," her voice is softer than the sound of the raging ocean and crashing waves, "that the dolphins come here to play." Her hand is small and elegant as she indicates the calmer water beyond the rocks. "You can wait with me if you like."

"That would be great. I was left behind last night. They are all so young and can't be bothered with me. I don't blame them. They have better things to do than babysit an oldie like me. I was pretty frightened. Didn't know what to do, then I found you and ..." I stop mid-sentence. She hasn't reacted to my words. It's like I'm not here at all. She picks up her camera and trains it on the ocean. I peer into the glare, but see no dolphins. She takes a series of photos, of the waves, of the gulls.

"And then I saw you and I thought about ..." I stop talking.

"You're such a blurter." There's my mother, sitting on the couch in the lounge room, after I found Steve and Sandy snuggled together in a coffee shop, alliteration hanging in the air around them. *"You keep spewing out all this information as if someone cares. You have to get over yourself. So, Steve's been having coffee with his secretary. That doesn't mean anything."*

I stop talking and look at Grace. I've heard someone call her Grace at the hostel. There are lines around her eyes, and a tinge of grey, small delicate lines of grey beginning to show in her hair. I've not noticed before. She looks older than I thought, older than me.

So I sit with her. I begin by fidgeting with the laces of my shoes. My head's still foggy, a dull ache along with the sharp pain at my temple. I lie back and close my eyes. I step aside from the world for a short time and re-enter it when the sun is directly above. As far as I can tell she hasn't moved. I stand up and walk to the edge of the cliff. I pace across the clearing. I sit again.

She is still. She hands me half a sandwich, a share of her water, a small handful of grapes. She smiles when I try to refuse half her lunch and pushes it towards me. Then I sit with her and watch the waves for any evidence of dolphins.

I don't mind the waiting. We don't talk, but somehow that seems the most natural thing. The day disappears as our silence grows. The ocean darkens. We sit and wait for dolphins.

...

The lights are bright in the hostel dining room. They make a fuss of me. Tell me how worried they were, laugh at me and laugh with me. I join in and joke around. "I could have been out there dying and decaying for all you cared," I say. "We knew you'd be okay," they say. "You're old and experienced." Then I take my dinner and sit at the table with Grace. I find that I don't mind sitting off to the side in silence.

"There might be dolphins tomorrow," she says. "You can come with me if you like."

...

It's blue, that sky. The waves so insistent on that lonely, long stretch of beach. I sit up and look right into the waves, shielding my eyes with my hand. If my mother was here she'd tell me I was wasting precious time, or that it was dull there on the beach, or that she can't stand the feel of gritty sand on her skin. I'd tell her that I like it. I peer into the waves in the hope of catching a glimpse of a grey, sleek body streaking through the water and darting out into the air to twist and turn and dive back beneath the surface. Alive. Skin tingling. Ready to jump again.

www.ingramcontent.com/pod-product-compliance
Lightning Source LLC
Chambersburg PA
CBHW070352120726
47909CB00008B/2821